MW01613284

Lady
Madeline's
Folly

LADY MADELINE'S FOLLY

Joan Smith

CHIVERS PRESS
BATH

British Library Cataloguing in Publication Data available

This Large Print edition published by Chivers Press, England, 1994.

Published by arrangement with the author.

U.K. Hardcover ISBN 0 7451 1947 6

Chapter 1

Lady Madeline Morash sat in her elegant saloon on the south side of St. James's Square, flipping impatiently through a thick stack of white cards. She displayed no enthusiasm for any of the balls, routs, dinners, levees, ridottos, or assemblies to which she was bidden in the coming weeks. After seven years on the town, she no longer found novelty in such entertainments. One ball was much like another after all. She was too much her father's daughter to find fulfillment in mere social doings.

Indeed that same Gold Saloon in which she sat was known in political circles as the Second Court of St. James. Decisions of national importance were as likely to be discussed there as at Westminster or 10 Downing Street, for her father, the Marquess of Fordwich, was a patriarch of the reigning Tory party. He had been a protégé of Pitt the Elder, his neighbor across the square in Chatham House. Pitt the Younger was spoken of in less glowing terms, after having snatched the prime ministership from under the nose of Fordwich in 1784. It was a hard blow, losing this top post to a youngster in his early twenties. Fordwich had held various senior positions in the party, but as he advanced into his seventies, he was content to be a minister without portfolio. He made his influence felt in the corridors of power in his role of wise old man of the party, advising, consulting, arranging strategies and compromises to confound the "demmed Whigs."

His daughter added her mite to the running of the country by acting his hostess, a role left vacant upon the death of his wife some years ago. Madeline was also his confidante, friend, companion, and sounding board for notions he intended to expound at Westminster. As she was a female, however, the larger part of her influence was felt in the social sphere, particularly that area of it lapping at the undefined boundary where the right contacts led to appointment or promotion. It was no secret a word from Lady Madeline, whispered in the right ear, could make the difference. Ministers, princes, royal dukes, ambassadors, committee chairmen, and board presidents—they were all her friends and callers.

Even as she sat deciding whether to honor the Countess Milthorpe's ball—a staid, formal, but highly prestigious do—or the less prestigious but infinitely more amusing rout party offered by the Gorringtons, the door knocker sounded to announce her first caller of the morning. She smiled with interest to see one of her old friends from the past enter.

"Lady Madeline, how nice to see you again!" The gentleman beamed as he advanced to pump her hand, which was extended to him. Curtsies were for young girls. Offering her hand, she felt, put her on a more equal footing with gentlemen callers.

"Captain Hopper, you are back from the wars. And not alone. Don't tell me this is a *wife* you have in tow?" As her eyes traveled over his shoulder to the shy-looking woman behind him, she realized it had better be a wife, for the lady was four or five months pregnant.

"As you see," he said with a nod, making

them acquainted. "I sent you an announcement of the wedding. Did you not receive it?"

She had no memory of it, though she received many such notices, and it had quite possibly slipped her mind.

"Ronald has told me so much about you," Mrs. Hopper said shyly. He had not happened to mention, however, that the lady who had been helpful in his promotion to captain was young and strikingly attractive.

Lady Madeline was tall. She held her head high, her body as straight as a soldier's. Her eyes were green, intelligent eyes, set in a pretty face framed by dark curls. She was vivacious, animated, which caused her to be considered more beautiful than she actually was. She was elegantly outfitted in a dark green morning gown, severely tailored, but lightened at the neck by a white collar and a silver filigree brooch.

"How many years has it been?" Madeline asked, ransacking her memory. Ronald Hopper had been one of her first projects, though not the very first. Her second season? No, the tail end of the first.

"More than six years, ma'am. A lot of water under the bridge since then. I fully expected to learn you were married. Audrey and I have a son—and a daughter, we hope, on the way."

"No, I am still single," she answered nonchalantly. She refused to be defensive in her replies to this frequently asked question. What could have given him the idea . . . ? Ah, Eskott, of course. She had been running around with Eskott that first season.

"Still in the business of helping needy callers, I hope?" he asked with a quizzing smile.

They sat down to a glass of wine and rehashed the past for several minutes. "So you are back from Canada, and looking out for a post, are you?" she asked bluntly.

"That's the idea," he admitted frankly.

"Do you have anything specific in mind?"

"I plan to leave the Navy. Some administrative post with the Admiralty occurred to me, after my years of experience."

"But why have you decided to sell out? The naval service is so active, expanding at this time. You should make quick progress up the rope, and you look very handsome in uniform, too," she added, with a smile to include his wife.

"Sailoring plays havoc with a man's private life," he said. "I was so much away from Audrey, you know. I am practically a stranger to my son. They were in Canada with me, but I did not see much of them, and would see even less if I got shipped off to help in the Peninsular campaign."

A closer examination of Audrey confirmed Madeline's suspicion that the woman was a clinging vine. Her social skills appeared to be nonexistent. She had scarcely opened her mouth since sitting down. There would be no raising Hopper any higher than she already had. Some quiet corner in the Admiralty could certainly be arranged, however. He spoke on about naval matters till she was quite bored with it.

"In particular I would be interested to do what I can to get the Orders in Council repealed," he told her, his eyes shining with zeal. "You have no idea how they are resented by the Americans. Even our own men don't like to be boarding and searching their vessels. It will lead to war in the end, if it isn't stopped. You may imagine how that would stretch our forces, already contending with Napoleon. I don't believe the folks at home have *any idea* of the territory we have to cover. From the northern wilds to Louisiana in the south, and from the Great Lakes to the mid-Atlantic. And what does it all accomplish in the end?"

"Why you begin to sound like a Jonathon, Captain Hopper. It accomplishes the goal of the laws passed in Parliament. Bonaparte has placed an embargo on English trade; England has retaliated by blockading countries that enforce Napoleon's Decrees."

"It does a deal of mischief. Our own manufacturers are as much against the orders as anyone. America buys a deal of their stuff, remember."

"I must confess I am not particularly well informed on the subject. Why don't you discuss your notions with the gentlemen at the Admiralty?"

"I intend to, but I would be listened to more sympathetically if I went with a letter from his lordship in my pocket. Everyone knows Lord Fordwich's influence."

She had some idea her father was in favor of the Orders in Council, and would not like to send Hopper spouting these opposing theories. She mentioned this in an oblique manner.

"Perhaps it is the Whigs I ought to visit," he said, disappointed. "They are against the Orders."

The word *Whig* was a red flag to her. What would they not give to have an experienced naval man declaring in no uncertain terms that he agreed with them, and why. "Let me see what I can do. I happen to know there is an excellent post vacant at Plymouth. What are your feelings about removing to Plymouth, Captain?"

"What sort of post is it? I plan to sell out and go into a non-military sort of work, you recall."

"Why give up your seniority and pension? It would be a desk job. You can keep your officer's pay but lead a settled life as well."

Ronald looked to his wife, whose eyes were shining with pleasure. "It would be lovely," she said wistfully. "You could still be near the ships and water, which you love so much, Ronald, but we could have a home too. A *real* home, our first."

"If you think you can arrange it . . ." Hopper said.

Lady Madeline smiled tolerantly. She was sure she could arrange it with the crooking of a finger. She discovered where the Hoppers were putting up—at a hotel whose name did not impress her—and smiled them out.

Within a minute, they were forgotten.

8

She was sorry to see Hopper had done so little with the opportunity she had given him. But then he had only been her second protégé. Her others had done better for themselves.

It was her custom each year to take under her wing a bright, young, upcoming gentleman who lacked connections, and sponsor him. Her first protégé had lately pleased her by being appointed as secretary to the Council of Penang. Another of her boys (she called them *boys* whatever their chronological age, though they were usually young) was about to head up the Parliamentary Committee on Corn. She had first got him elected M.P. for Tain Burghs, a small northern seat, but a clever man could make as much noise from a small borough as a large one, and even wield the same power as a county member who actually fought an election.

She had not yet found her boy for the coming season. That was why she was feeling so dull. It had nothing to do with Ronald's having a wife and child, and his surprise at finding her still single. She could have been married any time over the past years. Dozens of men had dangled after her most particularly. Several of them had spoken to her father, but she could not seem to care for any of them in a matrimonial way. Her interest in the wedded state was purely vicarious. She dabbled in the medieval pastime of matchmaking for others; for herself, the right man just did not seem to come along. Her own life was too interesting, too exciting—that was it. Why should she settle down to raise a brood of children, when she could be in the very center of the most exciting doings of the country?

She looked with interest toward the hallway at the sound of approaching footsteps. It was Lord Fordwich, who had just come out of his study, ready for his daily trip to Westminster. He had his greatcoat already about his shoulders, as it was December and a strong nip was in the air. In his hands he held a leather case, which would be stuffed with the papers he had brought home to study. He was tall, his once broad shoulders now beginning to stoop forward as he advanced into his seventies. He was still a commanding figure, however, with his full head of white hair swept majestically back from a high brow. His eyebrows had bristled with age, lending his countenance an angry hue that frightened new acquaintances but did not dismay his daughter in the least.

"Who was your caller?" he asked. "I heard some voices in the hallway a moment ago."

"Ronald Hopper. You remember him?"

"Ah yes, the youngster you got sent off to Canada. Back, is he? What has he to say for himself?"

"He mentioned selling out his commission and taking a job. I've promised to help him. I had in mind that post at Plymouth. Whom should I see about it, Papa?"

"That post is for an officer, Maddie, not a civilian."

"Oh, I talked him out of resigning. It is a settled life he craves—or his wife does. I had no opinion of her."

"I don't know why you bother your head with helping these thankless fellows—be better off with a brood of your own to mother. But for what it is worth, you might send him along to speak to Dundas—Robert Dundas. You can hardly send him to the First Lord of the Admiralty, what? Actually it looks as though Dundas will get the post soon."

"May I say *you* recommend Hopper?"

"I've heard no harm of the lad. Use my

11

name, if you think it will help. You are kind to trouble yourself on his behalf."

"It is not purely philanthropical. He spoke *against* those Orders in Council you have mentioned, you see. When I tried to straighten him out, he used that four-letter word we hate. *Whig!* Wouldn't they like to get hold of him? Plymouth is a good distance to put between him and Brougham and that set."

"Wise girl." He smiled approvingly. "The merchants are all up in arms over the orders."

"*Are* they a good measure, Papa? I felt ignorant about the subject when Ronald discussed it."

"Wise? Of course they are wise, unless you think we ought to let Bonaparte run tame over the seas. He has demmed near starved the nation with his decrees. Upstart!"

This superficial answer satisfied her. Her real interest in politics was small. She enjoyed being in the inner circle, and content to repeat the philosophies heard in her own saloon. Of greater interest was to watch the conflict of personalities, to prophecy who was a comer and who on his way out, who was clever and who stupid, who had the prince's ear this month and who was out in the cold, and best of all, who had outwitted the Whigs.

"Anything exciting scheduled for debate at the House today?" she asked.

"He's back. This may be it. I expect I'll be gone all day and half the night, Maddie." His eyes sparkled with excitement as he cast an arch smile in her direction.

There was no elucidation of the "he" necessary between them. "He" was Prince George, appointed regent the preceding February, when it was no longer possible to hope for his father's recovery from madness. "He" was no real favorite of Lord Fordwich. His high spending, his women, his drinking, and his running off to holiday at his Brighton pavilion at this time of crisis—all these could be overlooked. The great crime was that he was a Whig, almost certainly come back to London now to ask for Lord Perceval's resignation as prime minister, to set up that demmed Grey or Grenville in his stead.

"That sounds exciting. I'll go to the ladies' gallery and watch the show," Madeline decided.

"The excitement won't occur in the House," he told her, "but in private meetings. You would do better to stay home and receive callers. See what you can learn from them about the people's attitude to this change of power." But the truth was, there was seldom any but Tory callers in that house, and their attitude was as well known as an old ballad.

"Keep me informed," she said eagerly. "Send me a note the *instant* you hear anything definite. Perhaps I shall go to Almack's this evening and see what I can discover of Lady Hertford, or Yarmouth."

"You'll learn nothing from that pair," her father opined, but the young lady still had some hopes of charming the truth out of Lady Hertford's son, if not the prince's mistress herself.

The butler entered to inform Fordwich that his carriage was waiting. Madeline accompanied him to the door. She liked to watch his departures—his elegant body being bowed into his shiny black carriage, the horses jiggling in impatience to be off. There was a feeling of solidity and comfort in the knowledge that her father was one of the most powerful men in the country, and looked the part. But how old he was growing!

Just before she closed the door, he turned

back. "Oh, by the by, my cousin Aldred is sending his son to town—he should arrive today. He will call, no doubt. Make him welcome. He does not stay here, but is putting up with some friend."

Her mind flew swiftly over her cousins, scarcely recognizing the name, for the Aldreds were but little spoken of, in the usual way of poor relations. "Coming from where?" she asked.

"The north—Manchester. Looking about for a position, I believe. Aldred says he is a bright chap. You'll find something for him. I am too busy at this time. G'day." He nodded and was off, walking carefully, and being half hauled into his carriage.

Despite the excitement of a possible change of government, she continued thinking of her father when she returned to the saloon. Things would be very different when he died. Her position in society depended to no small extent on being Fordwich's daughter. She had no brother. Upon Fordwich's death, the title and estate would go to Cousin Morash, who was not at all active politically. It was even possible Morash would not welcome her at his home. Her mother's fortune of thirty thousand pounds was hers, so she would not be poor, but certainly her new establishment would not equal the one to which she was accustomed.

And if she bought a London home—and she could not envision a life without a London residence—would there be enough left over for a country seat? Never being able to leave the city except as someone's guest was nearly as dreadful an anticipation as not having a home in London. Cousin Morash would very likely offer her rack and manger, but his wife was a drab, dreary creature. What manner of social life would Cousin Eileen have, she wondered. The annual ball, for instance, might very well go by the board, as Eileen felt it her duty to present her husband a plight of her troth every year. Six children already she had encumbered him with, every one of them with red hair and freckles.

How *could* women do it? With a shake of her head, as though to get rid of the problem, she went to a desk and began penning her note to Robert Dundas, informing him that Captain Hopper . . . Her work was interrupted by a new caller. She looked up with interest as the butler announced: "Mr. Henry Aldred, ma'am."

Chapter 2

She looked up to see a sharp pair of brown eyes regarding her curiously. Henry's bow was graceful, if a trifle tardy. He had examined her longer than she liked. He was neither short nor ugly, and if he was poor, there was no real evidence of it in his appearance. The blue jacket that sat on his broad shoulders was not up to the quality of London tailoring, to be sure. A little bulge under the arms and a wrinkle at the shoulder were noticed upon a close inspection, but in the presence of Mr. Aldred, one's attention was more apt to be drawn to his person than his garments. He was tall, well formed, his face open and innocent without being rustic. The wind had turned his cheeks to scarlet, and the removal of his curled beaver had left one little strand of his dark hair hanging over his forehead, increasing his boyish charm. Yet he was clearly more than a boy—at least in his mid-twenties, she reckoned. There was an air of confidence on his ingenuous countenance that one did not see on younger faces.

"Cousin Aldred, delighted to make you

welcome," she said, offering her hand, like a gentleman. Aldred blinked in surprise, but stepped forward to grasp her fingers and give them a firm shake.

"Lady Madeline, delighted," he replied, as his eyes made a quick trip from the top of her fashionably tousled dark curls to the tips of her equally fashionable feet, clad in patent slippers. Neither was the lively face omitted, nor the graceful figure.

She took no objection to this scrutiny, occupied as she was in a similar examination of her caller. "I hope you left the family in Manchester well," she said politely, as though she were doing no more than making civil small talk. In fact, her every faculty was alert to judge his accent, his manner of expressing himself, his quickness. It was always amusing to annoy the ladies by appearing with a new escort.

"Tolerably well, thank you, ma'am. Papa tells me Cousin Fordwich is fine, and I can see there is nothing amiss with *your* health." This speech held just the proper amount of flirtation and admiration for a new young acquaintance of the opposite sex.

She smiled with satisfaction. "Do have

a seat, Mr. Aldred, and let us become acquainted. Such a pity we cousins grow up with never a peek at each other. It is always interesting to meet grown cousins for the first time, isn't it?"

"Not always so interesting as on this occasion," he replied with a gallant smile, as he accompanied her to the settee. He waited till she had arranged her skirts before joining her.

"Would you care for some coffee?" she asked. "I can see by your cheeks, and hear from that howling wind, that it is deuced cold out."

She judged correctly that the fleeting rise of his brow was caused by her using the word *deuced*. She enjoyed to shock provincial friends with her city expressions. "Thank you. That would be lovely. The fire looks tempting. Would you mind if I go to warm my hands?"

"Not at all. We'll sit closer to it, shall we?" She purposely walked a pace behind him, to observe him from the back. The shoulders were a little too padded, the waist nipped in more tightly than was fashionable. The hair too was cut shorter than that being worn by the urban bucks. These details were not only acceptable but welcome. There was no point in having a protégé if she could not help him, point out the little improvements, add the refining touches. Already it had darted into her mind that he would make an interesting protégé. The boots, she was happy to see, were unexceptionable. Much could be judged by a man's boots.

"Papa tells me you are putting up with a friend," she went on, in a spirit of conversational small talk that hid her rampant interest in him. "Would I be likely to know him?" She sat on one fireside chair, Henry on the other facing it.

"So he tells me," Aldred replied. "Taffy Barker, a friend from my university days. He says all of London knows Lady Madeline, and admires her." There was a glint of a smile in his eyes, a hint of admiration. He looked around the room as he finished his speech. The room too pleased him. It matched the woman—elegant, rich, good taste. He had learned that the correct method of proceeding was not to mention these things, however. To draw attention to them would imply a lack of familiarity. "How cozy this is," he said when he had finished his examination of the spacious chamber.

"Yes, we hardly use the larger rooms once the cold weather hits us. Taffy Barker, you say." Unexceptionable! To hear too that her cousin had been to university was encouraging. "That would be Oxford then, if I am not mistaken?"

"Yes, we were at Christ Church together a few years ago, and have kept up the acquaintance since, mostly through correspondence, but Taffy has also been to my home to visit me. It was his idea that I come to London."

"Is it to be more than a visit?" she queried, already knowing it was so.

"Yes, I am looking for a position. I am only a younger son, you must know, but I did not come here asking for help. I came to pay my family's respects to you and your father. Lord Fordwich is out, I take it?"

"Papa will not likely be home at all today. The prince regent has come back to town, you see."

"Oh," he answered blankly. "Your father is a good friend of the prince, is he?"

"Good God, no! Especially not at *this* time!"

"What is special about *this* time?" he asked.

Before long, Mr. Aldred was hearing

21

about the likelihood of the prince unseating the Tory party, and putting a Whig government in to rule instead.

"You seem very much interested in politics," he mentioned after a little talk.

"We live, eat, breathe, and sleep politics in this house, Cousin," she admitted readily. "But enough talk of *us*. What sort of work will *you* be looking for?"

"It is embarrassing to admit that after my years of university, I have not the least notion," he confessed. "I would have been wiser perhaps to have taken Holy Orders, or studied for some profession—the law or medicine." He sat thinking a moment. When he spoke, he said, "I wonder if there won't be plenty of opportunities for positions with the new government when it takes over. It stands to reason a new broom will sweep out a goodly number of the old boys."

Such an expression of interest in working for the opposition would have sent Lord Fordwich flying into the boughs. Lady Madeline was not the least distressed. It showed her he was wide awake, alive to an opportunity when he saw one. She would soon head him in the proper direction.

Before lunch was on the table, she had already begun dropping hints of so interesting a nature that Mr. Aldred had become half a Tory. Other comments revealed that so far as political principles went, he was not very well versed in partisan politics at all.

"Yes, no doubt there are opportunities on either side," he agreed over a raised pigeon pie, "but there is no advantage to aligning oneself with a party on its way out the door, if you see my meaning."

"There is many a slip twixt the cup and the lip, Mr. Aldred. The regent's main friend on that side of the house was Charles Fox. Now that he is dead, the inclination to change the government will not be so strong. Of course some of Prinney's best friends are Whigs—Lord Moira, Sheridan, Lord Hutchinson, and others. It is not *certain* he will depose Perceval, though he *does* hate him for his support of Princess Caroline."

"The regent's wife, you mean?"

"Yes, he took her side some years ago when the trouble developed between them. It has been a dreadfully unhappy marriage from the outset."

"The princess is extremely popular in the countryside," he told her.

"Well, she is not terribly popular here," she said stiffly. "Only the Whigs support her. We have more allies on our side. Lady Hertford, a great friend of the prince, and even the prince's own brother Cumberland, are by no means Whiggish. Never speak the words *Catholic Emancipation* before either of them. Then too, some of the Whigs wish to call off the Peninsular War, and I cannot think Prinney would like that."

"I personally believe Catholic Emancipation is long overdue, but as to the war, surely no man who calls himself an Englishman would speak of stopping now, when it seems Boney is pulling many of his troops out of the Peninsula. I hear rumors he is mounting a campaign in Russia."

She nodded in satisfaction to hear he was well aware of what passed around him, even if he had no particular interest in the government. Approving of Catholic Emancipation was tolerable—many of her father's crones did likewise. After lunch they returned to the grate in the Gold Saloon.

"You lead a very interesting life," Henry said, as she offhandedly mentioned various doings with the nation's most elite personages.

She smiled softly and began to reel him in. "Did it never occur to you to involve yourself in Tory politics, Mr. Aldred?"

"I am as ignorant as Paddie's pig in such matters," he confessed bluntly. "I haven't the connections for it, nor the financial backing either."

"I will undertake to arrange the connections. We are cousins, after all. I would be happy to do it, but the ignorance you must correct yourself."

"I am a fast enough learner. You are very kind, ma'am. I am convinced it would be a great bore for you, to have an unlicked cub like myself on your hands. Then too, there is the matter of money."

"I expect your credit is good. You cannot have done anything to destroy it. You've only arrived in town."

"I would not like to run into debt!" he said, aghast.

"It won't cost as much as you might think. We will find something that will keep you afloat for the nonce. Papa knows the ins and outs of the Civil List. You have some money, I expect?" she asked quite frankly.

"I am not completely destitute," he answered, showing a little pink around the collar at the open discussion of what was generally considered a private matter.

"Good. Use it wisely. Set yourself up in an elegant little apartment."

His eyes made a slow tour of the room he sat in. The ceilings, twelve or fifteen feet high, embossed with ornamental plaster medallions, the beautiful brocade draperies, the handsome and obviously expensive furnishings—all were encompassed in his look. "I could not afford much elegance," he decided wistfully.

"You won't need much, Cousin. A bachelor does not have to entertain at home. One decent room to greet your friends and associates is enough. Of course you'll need a bedroom and kitchen and so on, but they can be as spartan as you like. I'll help you find something. Your friend Taffy may have an idea what places are to let. We shall work something out. Come back to me tomorrow morning. Let me have a day to look into possibilities."

"You are very kind," he said. "Why should you go to so much trouble for me?"

"Why, we are cousins. What is family for, if not to take an interest in its members?" Her interest in this particular member was so high she wished to take him in hand at once, to begin that very evening taking him into society. But on this momentous night she must be at Almack's, where he could not enter in provincial tailoring, even if she could arrange a voucher on such short notice.

"I hardly know what to say. I did not come here to *beg*. I hope that is not your understanding."

"Rubbish! We are cousins, and will soon be fast friends. I look forward to seeing you tomorrow morning. I shall leave it free for you. Bring Taffy along, if you wish. Now I must be very rude and push you out the door. I am promised to a tea party this afternoon." This was not quite true, but she knew she might receive callers and did not wish to introduce her cousin to them yet, not till she had him brushed and polished and somewhat versed in the theories he would henceforth hold regarding the proper running of the country.

She smiled happily as the front door closed behind him. How exciting it was after all, having a new boy to sponsor. Such a charming, handsome young one, too! He put her other protégés in the shade. She must beware, or she would be setting up a flirtation with him. This was nonsense, of course. She always set up a flirtation with her boys, when they were single, as they usually were. It was quite a matter of course that they would fall head over heels in love with *her;* what was new in the situation was that the passion might, for once, be reciprocated. How high could Mr. Aldred not fly, with her considerable fortune and influence at his back?

The oddest thing about it all was that Cousin Aldred had not leapt at her offer to help. She sensed some little reluctance in him that intrigued her. He was a proud man, she thought, and liked him better for it.

"Lord Eskott, ma'am," the butler announced, disturbing her thoughts.

Her smile faded, to be replaced not with a frown but with a very calculating expression. It was not often a Whig passed through the portals of the Second Court of St. James. She must quiz him to see if he knew anything about Prinney's plans.

Chapter 3

"Show him in, Evans."

"Not necessary, Evans," Eskott said over the butler's shoulder as he lounged into the Gold Saloon, disregarding all the laws of polite behavior. Evans cocked his head aside and shook it, disclaiming any responsibility for this ill-behaved caller. The hostess took no offense; neither did she pay any particular heed to her guest's appearance. She was accustomed to his tall, rangy form, his severely elegant tailoring, his dark hair and eyes. She had not observed either when his summer complexion faded to winter's more subdued tone. She was only likely to comment on his appearance if he showed up without a fresh toilette, as he occasionally did after a hard day at the House. Today his appearance was unexceptionable, so she said nothing.

"Hallo, Maddie. Got yourself a new boy?" Eskott asked, pacing forward to sit beside her on the striped satin sofa, throwing one leg over the other. "I met a bright-eyed and bushy-tailed young provincial coming out as I entered. He called me *sir*, the whelp."

"Did you expect him to call you madame?"

"No, I didn't expect him to call me anything. We had not been introduced."

"How *encroaching* of him, to utter a civil good day to a stranger met on his cousin's doorstep!"

"Cousin, is he? I took him for your new boy." There was a mocking, jeering expression on the caller's face at this sally.

"Never mind that. You are no more interested in him than in the social gossip. What do you hear at Westminster?"

"That the old boys are to lose their posts. A black day for you, milady," he said with relish.

"Has he asked for resignations then?" she demanded instantly.

"Nope. He's called Grey and Grenville to meet with him. It looks as though Perceval is to be kicked out. That will give a good deal of satisfaction to Prinney, to repay him at last for supporting Princess Caroline."

"Who do you think will be offered the prime minister's post?" she asked, eyes sparkling. Eskott observed her, smiling.

"Prinney would like Moira, but there is no hope of it. Grey and Grenville would not sit still for it. Brougham, I suppose."

"What seat do you fancy for yourself, Eskott? The woolsack? You would like to be lord chancellor, I expect."

"I shouldn't mind being keeper of the national purse, but as the position includes as well keeper of the conscience, I may settle for a seat on the Treasury instead. I would not want such a heavy embargo on my soul as the conscience of the nation."

"I see you have been reviewing the duties of the chancellor all the same," she pointed out with a knowing smile.

"Gave myself away, did I?"

"Just so."

"I must set a seal on my tongue. You are too good a spy. Let us speak of less dangerous matters. Who is this cousin I met on the doorstep?"

She outlined Aldred's background, while Eskott listened closely. "I see it is your intention to take the lad in hand, but you must realize any friend of Taffy Barker is not likely to do you credit in any capacity but that of court clown."

"He is not at all like Taffy. He is intelligent—sharp."

"Also tall, handsome, and a bachelor. Don't omit the more stringent of your requirements in your boys."

She lifted her chin and tossed her head. "This has nothing to do with romance. It is business."

"I never met a lady under eighty who did not prefer conducting her business with a handsome gentleman. Young Aldred is tolerably pleasing in appearance," he added with lukewarm enthusiasm, regarding her all the while from the corner of his eye.

"He is *very* handsome!" she countered swiftly.

A conning smile peeped out on Eskott's dour face. "Not that you *care,* of course," he pointed out.

"You are perfectly horrid," she accused. "I don't know why I put up with you."

"Of course you do. You like to weasel Whiggish secrets out of me. No other member of my party is cork-brained enough to let you make a cake of him."

"True, and it serves you right, since you only come here to try to discover of *me* what Papa and the ministers are up to."

"That is not my primary reason for coming," he disagreed mildly. "We boast only one conversable lady in our ranks and Lady

32

Holland is half an outcast due to her divorce. It is my misfortune that the other two in the city are of the wrong political persuasion, but I visit both Melbourne House and the Second Court of St. James, despite that sad detail. I come for some lively female conversation, a glass of Fordwich's excellent sherry, and of course to admire your beautiful green eyes."

"When you begin on the beautiful green eyes, I know it is time to beware."

He shrugged. "Any chance of sampling the sherry?"

"I'll call Evans . . . and let him watch you pour yourself a glass," she finished, as he went to the wine table.

"We'll see if wine softens your hard heart, as flattery don't do it," he said, handing her a glass.

"You waste your time, Eskott. Papa is in conclave with the cabinet. I haven't the least notion yet what is going on. I have asked him to let me know as soon as anything happens."

"What is happening at the moment is that Prinney is with the Old Lady of Manchester Square, reading the Bible."

"What—with Lady Hertford at such a time?" she asked, frowning.

"It gives you a notion of how seriously he takes the situation, does it not?"

"At least he's not with Sheridan or Lady Holland, to have his reason perverted with your wrong-headed thinking."

"His new lady doesn't let him visit with Lady Holland, and would put Sherry on the interdict list too, if she dared. As to my perverted views, the reforms, electoral and otherwise, are not the perversion but the cure. There is too wide a discrepancy between the wealthy and the lower classes. We only want to share a little. The alternative, if you have read your French history, is revolution. You can't expect to keep ninety percent of the population in rags, without even a voice in Parliament, and not have them rise up in arms. How you can call *us* perverted astonishes me, Maddie. But you are too much your father's daughter to listen to reason, so I shan't preach."

"That's what our minister usually says after a long and tedious sermon—that he shan't preach."

"Which minister is that?"

"The *church* minister, idiot."

"Oh, *that* minister."

"Yes, I know you'd rather be quartered

34

with hot knives than visit a church, heathen."

"I have nothing against church, except that folks too often feel they have done their Christian duty once they have gone, and forget to practice what is preached."

After a little more chatter, he asked, "Shall I take you around to Almack's tonight? Should be a lively do, with Prinney back in town. Lots of new rumors to pick up."

"I'm not sure yet whether I shall go," she answered hesitantly.

"Aldred will not have had time to get a decent black jacket and knee breeches made up in one afternoon," he pointed out, with neither rancor nor offense. "Of course you will go. What you *mean* is that you are not sure you want my escort. I can take a hint, but you'll be sorry when you see me waltzing Lady Susan Glenn round," he warned, wagging a long, shapely finger at her.

"Lady Susan again!" she said, lifting her brows. "This becomes serious. You danced with her once last season, if memory serves." This was a facetious reference to Eskott's habit of dallying with all the ladies, while not encouraging any of them to the extent of a serious flirtation.

"Also the season before," he added.

"Yes, she has been on the town rather a long time, has she not?"

"Ages, nearly *half* as long as yourself, Maddie," he riposted.

"Wretch!" she laughed good-naturedly. "I am a confirmed ape leader. Pray do not put me in the same youthful category as the Lady Susans of the world."

"Is it impossible to bestir you to anger?" he asked lazily, with a rueful shake of the head.

"Not in the least. You can always infuriate me by implying I am trying to make a match with my protégés. Robbing the cradle, in fact."

"A very meager cradle too, for the wealthy Lady Madeline," he pointed out. "If you plan to rob a cradle, you might at least make a pass at Devonshire, or one of the other ducal cradles."

"That pup! He isn't a duke yet either, but only a marquess."

"*Only* a marquess, eh? That puts me in my place. What are you hanging out for then, a royal prince?"

"I am not hanging out for a husband at all. I have refused several excellent offers, as you well know."

"You keep reminding me of the fact. It has not wholly slipped my memory that one of the better offers was from myself."

"You are the one who brings it up. I don't know how it is we always end up discussing my marriage, when you really come here to pick my brains to see what I have learned from Papa."

"There must be some reason for it, I suppose," he replied reasonably.

Before he could say more, Lady Madeline diverted him with a completely new topic. "Where do you have your jackets made up, Eskott?"

"Weston. But he is too expensive for your country cousin," he told her with a sneering smile.

"Nonsense. No price is too high for such a well-fitted jacket."

"Better send him along then, or he'll discover Stutz, and have even more wadding stuffed into his shoulders than he already has. It is your intention to turn the sow's ear into a silken purse, is it?"

"Why yes, I am a famous magician in that respect. I usually perform one such miracle every season."

"You might pass your magic wand over his manners while you are about it."

"I come to think you could use a touch of it yourself. You are not usually so high in the instep, condemning a man for so little reason."

"If we can find nothing more interesting than Aldred to discuss, I shall take my leave and try my luck with Lady Holland instead. Good day, ma'am."

"Oh, Eskott, would you mind very much dropping my books off at the circulating library?" she said as he arose. "I am staying home today, in case of a note from Papa."

"A pleasure and a privilege, Maddie. Could I deliver any messages for you while I am about it? Polish your boots, fill you a tub for bathing? Groom your mount?"

"Thank you, dear Eskott. They are on the table in the hall. Evans will give them to you. Save me a dance if I go to Almack's." She wiggled her fingers at him and laughed.

A reluctant smile settled slowly on his lips as he stood looking at her. "There is not another lady in London who treats me so shabbily as *you* do. One of these days, milady, you shall pay the piper," he said with mock menace.

"How much do I owe you? Don't be shy to present your bill."

"Thirty thousand pounds," he answered cryptically.

She could make nothing of it, till she remembered it was the sum of her dowry. She wasted very little time thinking about it, for she had a lengthy list to make up if she was to transform her cousin into a buck of the first water.

Eskott had long since stopped being a suitor in her mind, and become a good friend. The offer of marriage, still occasionally mentioned, had occurred in her first season. At eighteen, she had been aware of the glory of having attached such a prime *parti* without feeling the least desire to become his wife. Not wishing to lose his friendship, she had couched the refusal in polite but unencouraging terms. It had been accepted with no evidence of hard feeling or heartbreak on the gentleman's part. They continued to frequent the same parties, standing up together for a dance, meeting several times a week at one do or another. About three years later, they began going out occasionally for a drive or visit together, as friends, and no more. His calls at the Second Court of St. James had resumed that year, and had increased in frequency since, but there was little gallantry in him. The intimacy between them had become something like a familial affection.

Madeline was never seen to bat her eyes at him over a fan, to either glare or poker up or increase her attentions to another beau on those frequent occasions when he escorted other ladies about town or took up with a new dasher. She had long since taken to herself the matron's privilege of teasing all the gentlemen about their *chères amies*. Eskott was roasted along with the rest, with the same frank jocularity and good nature.

No formality lingered. If she needed an escort, she asked him to accompany her. If he could not comply, she was not at all put out. She used him to perform errands and small jobs for her, but was equally help-ful in relieving him of certain duties that were unpalatable or impossible for a bach-elor. She quite often made up his guest lists for balls or parties, advised him how best to amuse visiting maiden relatives, or amused them for him if he was too busy. It was a very agreeable friendship, which she had not the least intention of losing, or changing in any way. She would sorely miss Eskott if he dropped her, but that was not even remotely likely in her view.

She returned to her desk and drew out a clean sheet of paper. She inscribed Henry's name at the top, and began listing his requirements:

1. Suitable residence (cheap)
2. Toilette—jackets, evening clothes, gloves (see Taffy Barker)
3. Clubs—non-gambling
4. Transportation.

Did he have a decent mount, carriage, money to provide them if he had not? She soon realized that Henry's largest need was for money to provide these necessities.

As she began listing possibilities, she remembered Captain Hopper, and completed the note to Robert Dundas. She stuck it beneath the list, and forgot it. A new protégé often had this effect of making her forget trivialities, and even of shrinking duties assumed to the inconsequence of trivialities, in her mind.

Chapter 4

The meetings and rumors of a new government continued over the next week, but as nothing definite was accomplished, Lady Madeline was free to begin her transformation of Mr. Henry Aldred. Lord Eskott, who ran into him more than once on St. James's Street, cast a blighting stare on the young man, and was at pains to make him look uninformed, which was not difficult in those early days.

Aldred had been accompanied by Taffy Barker when he appeared at Lady Madeline's door for his second meeting. Barker was a town beau whose sole accomplishment was that he was "up to all the rigs," in a social sense. He had not managed to squander the fortune left him by his father, nor to alienate the large circle of friends his mother's predominant social position entitled him to. He went to all the right parties, and a good many of the wrong ones. He drove a snappy yellow curricle harnessed up to a prize pair of grays; he was turned out by Weston, belonged to the best clubs, and was accepted everywhere. That was about the sum and total of his life. He was tall, painfully thin, and noticeably ugly, with a face as narrow as a razor blade. What he admired most in other people was a handsome appearance. With such lax requirements in his giving of friendship, he was frequently taken advantage of. Lady Madeline had every intention of imposing on his good nature to help her turn Henry out in style.

"Lady Madeline, always a pleasure," he said as he entered her saloon.

He was greeted with no more than a fleeting smile. The lady's interest was on her cousin. How handsome he looked beside Taffy! Better than she had remembered. And how poorly outfitted! *Worse* than she remembered.

"How are you enjoying your visit, Cousin?" she inquired, pointing to a pair of chairs facing her.

"Very much indeed. Taffy is showing me the sights. We took in a visit to Jackson's Boxing Parlour yesterday afternoon, and a play last night. We have just come from the Daffy Club—a famous place for members of the Fancy."

She nodded, having no interest in these things, but only in getting on with his lessons. Taffy felt obliged to inquire for Lord Fordwich and a few of Madeline's relatives, which prompted her to ask for the health of his mother and sister. This done, she got down to business. Had Aldred given any thought to her suggestion in the matter

of his career? Indeed he was greatly interested, but could not like to impose on her
good nature, and her time.

"Not *just* her good nature. Lady Madeline's hobby horse," Taffy mentioned. "Be
a jolly good thing for you, Henry. The mak-
ings of you. Lady Madeline's fellows always
advance on the double."

Henry looked interested enough that she
continued. "The first item of business will
be to find you suitable lodgings."

"Welcome to stay with me," Taffy offered.

"You are very kind," Madeline said, "but
it will not do in the long run. Your mama
and sister will not like to have a permanent
house guest who is no kin or connection
to the family."

"Mama won't mind. Mary will be delighted." Mary, who bore a strong physical
resemblance to her brother, never minded
having a gentleman forced into her orbit.

"Mr. Aldred will require privacy for his
work," Madeline said to put an end to this
scheme. "Now about an apartment, I think
the Albany, don't you, Taffy?"

"Only place for bachelors," he agreed.
"Top of the trees. Good handy location.
Not dear either."

"Do you happen to know if there are any vacancies?" she inquired, despite an air of dissatisfaction that rested on Henry's features.

"Happens I do. Bricklin flew the coop two days ago. Owed a quarter's back rent. In the basket. Left his belongings there. Seized by the bailiff for rent. Be happy to rent the place furnished. Nice stuff too: Sheraton set of chairs, marble-topped commode, good mahogany writing table. Dashed hard bed—could put a feather tick on it. Do the whole thing up brown for a monkey."

"Excellent," Madeline said. "You must go there today and hire the place, Cousin."

"I am not accustomed to living in hired rooms," Mr. Aldred exclaimed. "I would much prefer to rent a cottage."

"Too steep," Taffy told him.

"A shabby little cottage is not at all the thing for you," Madeline agreed. "Better a little elegance than a lot of squalor."

"I shall be having company. My mother plans to visit me, and also friends from home. A small flat will not do at all."

"The address is very important," Madeline explained. "The Albany is so well located, right at Piccadilly."

"Have a look at least," Taffy urged.

"All right, I'll *look,* but I favor a private house," Aldred said after repeated urgings from his two mentors.

The next step was more difficult to accomplish. It is no easy thing to tell a gentleman his clothing is rustic. When he is clearly halfway up into the boughs already, a certain degree of discretion is necessary. "What a handsome jacket you are wearing, Taffy," she began judiciously.

Taffy opened his lips and smiled in pleasure. "Never put myself in any hands but Weston's," he admitted.

"He is the *only* tailor favored by the ton, I believe," she said casually. "There is no matching him."

Henry was by no means so slow as to overlook her meaning. "I suppose I ought to visit him, if I am to rub shoulders with the sort of people you have been speaking of," he said, much to her delight.

"Suit yourself," was her mild encouragement. "I must say, if *I* had such a fine figure, I would wish to show it off to best advantage."

In this flattering and insinuating manner, the conversation continued. Taffy extolled the virtue of Hoby as bootmaker. "A man

46

daren't be shod by anyone else. The king, the prince regent, Duke of Kent, Wellington. Top of St. James's Street, next to the old Guards Club. I'll introduce you. Baxter is your man for curled beavers."

He also suggested where shirts and cravates and other necessities could be obtained. "I daresay it will cost me a small fortune," Henry objected.

"No, a large one," Taffy countered.

"It need not be paid for all at once," Madeline pointed out.

"Put 'em on tic," was Taffy's more straightforward advice. "No one pays cash on delivery. I'll let 'em know you're to be trusted. Mind, you must put a little something on account from time to time. Another thing, if you mean to cut a swath in society, you'll need a new carriage."

"All this can't be necessary only to get a position!" Henry objected. "I must draw the line somewhere. My little whiskey is good enough." A belligerent set to his chin told his mentoress she had accomplished enough for one day. He would soon see for himself, as he went about with a more elevated, citified crowd, that a whiskey was not at all good enough, and for the meanwhile, it was her own landau that would take them for drives in the park, and her father's carriage that would deliver them to balls and plays and the opera. She did not mean to disdain the social gatherings by any means. They were her main means of meeting the right people, or letting the right people meet her current protégé at least.

"What sort of work do you have in mind for me, Cousin?" Aldred asked.

"I must know you better before I decide. What is your strength? Writing letters, meeting and dealing with people on a personal basis, organizing affairs, studying a project and writing a report? If it is the foreign service that interests you, then I must know what languages you speak."

"Only English, with of course Latin and Greek, but that is of no account. My French is indifferent. I understand it, but speak it poorly. I write business and facts well enough, but am not at all poetical."

"There is very little poetry in the sort of writing I speak of," she informed him.

"I get along pretty well with most folks," he added, after a little further considering.

"Best-liked fellow at Christ Church," Taffy augmented.

"That is high praise indeed!" Madeline

exclaimed. "Perhaps it is some position dealing with the public that would best suit you."

"I would prefer that to sitting alone writing up reports," he said with great feeling.

"I must introduce you to some of the upper echelon of the party, and see how you get on with them. I'll brief you first as to their little idiosyncrasies, and their particular areas of interest," she offered. "I'll discover from Papa which of the members are short-staffed as well. I expect you will want a position immediately, as money is tight. The first job need not be the last, remember. What are you doing tonight, Taffy?" she asked, turning to include the other caller in the conversation.

When he mentioned a snug little dinner at one of his clubs, followed by a hand of cards, she took the opportunity to caution Henry against heavy gambling. "There is no worry there," he reassured her. "Gambling does not run in our family."

On the whole, she was satisfied with the visit. Henry was definitely not so biddable as her other protégés, but this only made her job more of a challenge. When the gentlemen returned properly outfitted for going into her sort of society, she would drop Taffy and take Henry firmly under her own wing.

Beyond her door, one of the callers was less than satisfied. "She's a demmed managing female," Aldred said with a scowl.

"Most managing female in London," Taffy agreed readily. "The most competent to manage, too," he added. "Her fellows always get advanced on the double. Told you so. She'll have you a minister before the decade is out. Stick with a winner, Henry."

Henry regarded him, frowning. "I am not averse to getting some new jackets. I need them in any case, but I'll be a monkey if I'll hire rooms at the Albany just because Lady Madeline Morash says so."

"Shall we have a look all the same, to satisfy her?" Taffy asked.

"We might as well have a *look*, but I don't mean to dance to her tune."

The suite lately vacated by Mr. Bricklin, when it was examined, proved so nicely got up, so really convenient considering its small size and price, so close to what was likely to be Aldred's place of work, that in the end it seemed foolish not to take it.

"The money I save will be more than

enough to put Mama and . . . and any visitors I may have up at a hotel when they come," he pointed out to Taffy.

"Yes, by Jove," Taffy agreed. "Foolish to have a whole house standing idle, when Agnes won't be spending more than two weeks in London, if she comes at all."

"It is not Agnes I am worried about. It is Mama," Aldred insisted.

"Certainly your mama must chaperone her. No one else. Mean to say, can't have a young lady hopping about London with you unchaperoned. Hasn't any mother of her own. Old Uncle Leadbeater could come with her, but he is too old to relish the trip. Besides, he don't favor your suit. Doubt he'll let her come at all. Really no point hiring a house."

"Leadbeater has no objection to myself. It is only my lack of a fortune or position that he dislikes. If my cousin can help me find a lucrative post, then there will be no objection to the match, I fancy."

"I wouldn't mention Agnes to Lady Madeline just yet if I was you, Henry."

"Why not?" he asked.

"She won't like the notion of you thinking of marriage, when she is working on your career. She'll see it as too much distraction for you. Besides, there's nothing definite set between you and Agnes."

"I was turned off, but as Leadbeater said Agnes might come to London with Mama for a few weeks . . . Well, I don't think he is unalterably opposed, though he has told me not to hope. Agnes too has told me I must consider myself quite free."

"That's good then. Madeline will expect you to be her *cavalier,* in payment for her efforts on your behalf. Have to do the pretty, my boy. Let her drag you along to parties to show you off. Far as that goes, she'd be a great catch, if the thing with Agnes don't work. She don't equal Agnes in guineas and pence, but she's got a tidy fortune at her back. Good family connections too."

"She wouldn't look twice at a provincial like me. I never much cared for older women anyway, to tell the truth. *I* prefer to wear the trousers in my house. Whoever she marries, she'll have him petticoated inside of a month."

"Doubt that. At least if Eskott ever gets a ring around her finger, she won't keep *him* tied to her apron strings. Daresay that's why she won't have him. Ain't biddable enough. Still, I reckon the right man could tame her."

Aldred turned his head to look Barker in the eye. He opened his mouth to argue, then closed it again without speaking. Later he said, "About the jackets, Taffy, do you think Bath cloth?"

This intriguing question occupied their attention for the drive to Old Bond Street.

Chapter 5

Lady Madeline's friends received their first tantalizing glimpse of Mr. Aldred the day he called on his mentor sporting his new jacket.

"You do Mr. Weston proud," she complimented him, her eyes flickering over his broad shoulders, approving the more sedate buttons than those he had worn previously. His somewhat garish flowered waistcoat had been tamed down to one of narrow stripes. The only matter in need of improving was his barbering, and hair could not be expected to grow to a proper length in half a week, even to please Lady Madeline. She suspected that if she could hint him into brushing it forward in the Brutus do, however, it would look much better. The question was—how to accomplish it without hurting his feelings.

"Certainly you are as modish as Mr. Beau Brummell himself," she rattled on. "Why, if only your hair were brushed forward as he wears his, no one could tell the two of you apart."

Taffy Barker, who was familiar with the diminutive dandy spoken of, started at so unlikely a comparison, but Henry was familiar only with the name, and knew it for the top of the trees. He cast a knowing eye on his cousin, held her gaze for a long moment, challenging her. They both broke into a smile at the same time.

"Your dilemma, I see, is to get my hair forward without getting my back up," he said.

"Precisely! Do let's try it. Taffy, have you a comb?"

Taffy was as well supplied as a lady with the accoutrements of fashion. He not only had a comb in his pocket, but performed the task required. When he had finished, Madeline took the comb from him to put the finishing touches on the coiffure herself. She smiled softly, to see Henry's cheeks suffuse with color at this intimate task. The

54

curls arranged to her satisfaction, she took his arm and walked him to the mirror. "Now, tell me I was right," she ordered.

He gave one quick, disparaging look at his image and turned away. "I look like a sissy," he mumbled, but he seemed resigned to the change.

"You look extremely handsome. In fact, I want to show you off. Will you drive with me in the park?"

"Taffy has his sporting carriage. We came in it. It only holds two," Henry explained.

"Taffy won't mind if I borrow you for a few hours, will you, dear Taffy?" she asked with a conning smile. "I'm sure he has something else he can do."

Taffy was sensitive enough to realize he had been hinted out of her carriage, which could carry the three of them very easily, with room to spare. "Matter of fact, I have to settle up at Tatt's today," he answered readily.

To reward him, she invited him to join a waltzing party she had arranged for later in the week. This new dance was not yet accepted at such prudish establishments as Almack's, but it was gaining momentum, whirling merrily at the edges of society. When it was done by everyone, there would be no cachet in performing it. Lady Madeline liked to be in the front lines of fashion. Henry, of course, was invited as well.

In the park, she had her carriage stopped at the barrier, to present a few select persons to her cousin. The response to him, most particularly the feminine response, was all she could have wished for. She let him preen and smile, till one of the bolder girls invited him to call on her, at which time she remembered she had to rush home and write a few letters.

"What are you and Taffy doing tonight?" she asked, as he left her at her door.

"I shan't tell you. You won't like it," he replied with a teasing smile.

"Gambling?" she asked swiftly.

"No. Taffy is presenting me at the Green Room, at Covent Garden," he answered boldly. "All we debs have to make our bows, you know, Cousin. A brushing acquaintance with the demimonde is part of a gentleman's education. It is kind of you to sponsor my worthier pursuits, but a man needs some fun too."

"So you don't enjoy my company," she returned, in the same teasing spirit. If he had thought to scandalize this seasoned lady, he was sadly out. The only surprise in it was that he should be making his bows at so late an age. This was more normally done during university days.

"Certainly I do. And I appreciate your efforts too, even if I have been a savage in the matter of rendering proper thanks."

"You are coming along very nicely," she replied, patting his fingers as though he were a child.

"I have an excellent teacher. Also a very pretty one," he said with a bow. Then he raised her fingers to his lips and touched them before taking his leave.

She was happy with his progress in his dual duties of refining himself and developing his amatory techniques. She sent out notes to her waltzing party, arranged for musicians and a dancing master. On the day of the party, she received, along with her usual stack of invitations, a brief note from Captain Hopper, asking if she had had any response from her inquiries on his behalf. Chagrined, she tried to remember whether she had ever gotten around to actually posting the letter she had written. After searching her desk, she discovered she had not. She dashed off another, mentioning there was some urgency in the matter, and set it aside for her father to frank when he returned. Then she gave herself over to preparations for the dancing lesson.

She remarked, as her guests came trickling in, how her friends from the past had changed. The girls with whom she had made her debut seven years ago had aged dreadfully. Anna had put on ten or twenty pounds, and Isabelle looked a positive frump. It was marriage and raising a family that did it, she supposed, but was annoyed with them all the same. She was happy she had included some younger ladies, met over the years as they were presented. One of these bold chits took the idea she would be Henry's partner in the dancing lesson, till Lady Madeline took her firmly by the arm and handed her over to Taffy Barker.

"I've tried this a few times before, Henry," she said. "I shall give you the benefit of my experience." The use of first names had been established the day before, during one of his visits.

"You are very kind. And after I have had the benefit of your experience, I should like the benefit of an introduction to the *charming* young lady you have handed over to Taffy. You forgot to introduce us, Madeline. Something new, for *me* to be giving *you* a lesson in propriety."

"You would not be interested in her. She is practically engaged to another fellow. Are you looking about for a wife?"

"Not at all, but most of the ladies at your do are older," he said, looking over the selection with very little interest.

The dancing master, a clamorous Italian, called the class to order, making it unnecessary for her to reply. The party was not so enjoyable as she had hoped. Anna Willoughby asked her who "the young fellow" was.

"My cousin," she replied, disliking the emphasis on *young*.

"I was sure he must be. It is kind of you to have thrown a party to introduce him to a few of the coming debs, but I cannot think it necessary. Taffy will be sure to parade them all before him. Has he any fortune?"

"Nothing significant."

"Pity."

Eskott chose that day for one of his fleeting, unannounced visits. He arrived after the lesson was over, and the guests were refreshing themselves with tea. He took one look into the room and turned to leave, but Madeline spotted him and waved. As he still did not enter, she went to him.

"My feelings are in tatters. Why was I not invited to this interesting debauch?" he asked.

"I made sure you would be much too busy laying snares to trap your enemies."

"How is the sow's ear coming along?" he asked, scanning the throng for Henry.

"Judge for yourself," she replied, nodding her head in his direction.

"I see you have got him into a well-tailored jacket at least. Now if only you could lighten that unfortunate country complexion—or is he blushing? Yes, I do believe the chit with him is flirting her head off."

She looked quickly to see what girl her cousin was with, and felt a definite pique to observe it was the one he had complimented earlier. "They are all running mad for him," she said airily. "But then he is very handsome."

"Handsome is as handsome does."

"How *do* you invent these original phrases? Don't forget to mention that clothes make the man."

"I can't agree with you there, or I would have to admit we were both made by the same maker. Have you got him a position yet?"

"No, but he's about ready now. Can I get you some tea?"

"Not this time. I didn't realize you had company. I'll dash along and check my snares." He bowed and left, and Madeline darted back to Henry. She was just in time to hear him explain to the girl that he would offer to drive her home, but unfortunately he didn't have his carriage with him.

"Of course, if you had set up a decent carriage as I told you to, you could have had the pleasure of taking Miss Armitage home," she told him after the girl left. It was some consolation when he agreed, reluctantly, that he really needed a carriage.

With Taffy's help, he soon had one. Within ten days of his arrival in London, he was indistinguishable from a gentleman who had been on the town for years. More importantly, he was quick to grasp the nuances of his future career. He could speak with the informed now about the prince's tardiness in throwing out the Tories and bringing in his old friends, the Whigs, from the wilderness of the opposition. This was seen as an excellent sign.

"It looks very hopeful for our chances," he commented to Lord Tilsit, whom he met in Lady Madeline's saloon one morning.

"It is," Tilsit agreed, "but then he will not come into full powers till February. The Regency Bill has him tied wing and leg for the duration of a year. Come February, I fear we will see the change."

"I do not despair by any means," Fordwich countered. "He has the power now to be rid of us if he wished. We can count on the total support of Lady Hertford and her set. They carry a good deal of influence with him."

"Too much," Tilsit said with a sagacious nod.

"What do you think of this notion of making up a cabinet including some of the more illustrious Whigs, combined with our own brighter luminaries, in the manner of the old Government of All the Talents?" Aldred asked. "Yourself Lord Tilsit, and Lord Fordwich of course," he added.

This piece of flattery was not taken amiss. "Harumph," Tilsit said, "he only wants Sheridan and Moira out of the Whig camp, if the truth were told. If we could convince that pair to join us, the matter would be settled, but one might as well expect a fish to fly."

"In the case of Sheridan, the fish is more likely to drink than fly," Madeline said. "He was completely foxed at the theater last night."

"As to that," her father opined, "birds of a feather roost together. The prince is now taking a deal of laudanum as well as wine, from what I hear."

"But do you think the Whigs would agree to a combined cabinet?" Aldred asked, taking every interest in these esoteric details.

"Not with Perceval driving the coach," Fordwich said with strong feeling. "They would not sit still for it, so what's the point of conjecturing? They loathe and despise the man. So does the prince, of course. My own feeling is that one-half of our problem is Perceval. If we had a different prime minister than the prince's old enemy, there would be no more talk of throwing us out."

"Why does no one hint to Perceval that his resignation would be acceptable?" Aldred inquired, mystified. "Surely he must put the good of the party before his own career?"

"Who will enter the lion's den on such an errand?" Tilsit asked in a rhetorical spirit, for he knew no one would, including himself.

Fordwich could not long remain with his guests. A page came from Westminster with a dispatch box. "I had best look this over in private," he said, excusing himself.

When he was gone, Tilsit turned to Aldred. "You take a keen interest in politics, sir," he began. "It is encouraging to see the younger generation so well informed. If you should decide to go the next step and enter the fray, call on me. I could use a bright young man at this busy time. In fact, there may be a seat coming up in one of the boroughs I control."

Madeline's face lit up with delight. She glanced at Henry, who was regarding Lord Tilsit, his expression undecided. "That is very kind of you, sir," she said, when Aldred failed to make any verbal answer. "My cousin is indeed interested in becoming actively engaged in politics."

"Good. Then I look forward to seeing you soon. Now I must be off. Good day."

When he was gone, Madeline turned to Aldred, annoyed by his lack of enthusiasm at the offer. "Why did you not get it settled at once?" she asked.

"He mentioned a seat, my becoming an M.P. That would cost a great deal, waging a campaign, and then there is no money in it either."

"It wouldn't cost you a penny. The seat

he spoke of is a rotten borough, consisting of a barn and a couple of hen houses. It is his to give. There would be no expense."

"No, nor any salary either, after it has been accomplished. He is looking for a free clerk."

"My dear boy," she said, shaking her head at his naiveté, "there are perquisites aplenty. An appointment to some position in the royal household could be arranged, to give you an annuity without increasing your workload a cubit. It is done all the time."

"It is not done by the opposition, but by the government. It is unclear yet that our party will remain long in power."

"Better take it now then, while they *are* in power, to make the appointment. For that matter, Tilsit first mentioned a different sort of job. He said he could use some help—a sort of secretary I expect is what he had in mind."

"That is more interesting at the moment."

"Go to see him then, today. Don't waste a moment."

"I don't know that I would like being a secretary, to spend my days crouched over a desk, composing letters."

"You can hardly expect to start at the

top, Henry. It is like anything else; you must work your way up."

"I shall think about it."

"Good. I want you to think about something else too. Christmas. We are going home to Highgate Hall for the holiday. I would like you to join us. We are inviting a party of *very influential* people whom it would be helpful for you to know. The Castlereaghs will be there, Liverpool, and others. We leave three days before Christmas, and return at the start of the new year."

"I had planned to go to my own home for Christmas," he told her. "It is very kind of you, but my family will be expecting me, you know, and I cannot like to disappoint them."

"I assume they are reasonable. They sent you to London to find a position. They will not expect you to throw this excellent opportunity away, only for a family visit. Go and visit them *after* you have got yourself established, Henry. You must make a few sacrifices for the sake of your career."

None of her other protégés had hesitated to grasp the plums she held out to them. Yet there was some merit in his objection. He needed money, so a fairly demanding job with no salary was not the best one for him. Court appointments took time and were uncertain now, with the government's fate in the balance. For a son to wish to spend Christmas with his family was hardly to be condemned either, even though it was unwise. He was a curious blend of the sentimental and the practical, she decided. And whichever side he showed her, she found it attractive. She liked to go out in public with him, and watch her friends stare. She knew Henry was attracted to girls. She saw how his lips lifted when they cast their sheep eyes at him. It always angered her, and intrigued her too that he did not step up his courting of herself.

He was unfailingly polite, a *little* gallant, but he was not smitten. He casually mentioned outings with other women, without looking to see if she minded. Perhaps that was his greatest charm for her; that she was not certain of him.

She occasionally mentioned finding him a well-dowered wife, to remove the burden of his lack of funds. She even had her eye on a few suitable heiresses, but was curiously reluctant to put them forward. Her Christmas party, for instance, could very well include Miss Anita Gresham and her mama, but she had no real intention of inviting them. She looked forward to the party with a good deal of pleasurable anticipation. There would be time to get to know Henry better, more intimately, to spend some hours with him at pursuits other than career-oriented ones.

"I shall write to Mama, but if she *insists,* you know, Maddie, I cannot disappoint her."

"Your sentiments do you credit, but if she is as wise and as interested in your future as I think she is, she will urge you to come to Highgate with me."

"Don't count on it. She likes to keep me tied to her apron-strings. She has that in common with you, Cousin."

"Well, upon my word, is *that* what you think of me?" she asked, too surprised at first to take offense. "Have I ever demanded an accounting of your time—your evenings, for example? I assure you, my *only* interest in you is to see you respectably established."

"But what is in it for *you?*"

"It is my hobby, avocation, if you like. It is enjoyable to have friends in various careers, doing all manner of different and interesting jobs. I keep in touch with my fledglings after they have flown the nest. Why you sound as though I were . . ."

He looked at her narrowly; then a reluctant smile peeped out. "You must think me a dashed conceited fellow. I certainly did not mean to imply you were dangling after me. I know well enough Lord Fordwich's daughter with a dowry of a hundred or so thousand pounds would not be casting her cap at a mere nobody like myself."

"You overestimate both my dowry and your own worthlessness, Henry. I have only thirty thousand to call my own, and you are an intelligent, educated young man, in whose *career* I take a *cousinly* interest."

He lowered his head and look chastened. "I'm sorry. I spoke out of line. Can you forgive me?" She hunched her shoulders and dismissed it with a smile.

He arose and moved to a chair closer to her. "What *really* bothers me, you know, is that I . . ." She gazed at him with curious fascination, noting the shy shadow that was in his eyes. "Oh, damme, Madeline, it is no secret that every man you take an interest in falls in love with you on the spot. You are so beautiful, so charming, so self-assured, so far above us earthbound mortals, like a star shining in the sky. I don't want to have my heart smashed and tossed over your shoulder, like all the others. If I have been a little reluctant to be led by you . . . well, that is the reason." He looked at her, uncertain.

"That is a very good reason. I promise I shan't smash your heart, Cousin," she said with a teasing smile.

"I'm sure you never do it on purpose," he answered gallantly.

"Perhaps I have a solution to the problem. I shall invite some eligible young ladies to our Christmas party. Miss Gresham, I believe, would make an excellent heart-smasher for you."

"No, no. If it is to be smashed at all, I would like to have it done by the best. You."

"Miss Scott has a dot of—"

"Please!" he said, raising a hand to ward off her suggestion. "I have no intention of marrying a fortune for the sake of a fortune. Should I find myself in love with a lady of means who was inclined to have me, that would be a different matter. I suppose it would be foolish to let that stand in the way of making an offer, but I refuse to become a gazetted fortune hunter. I despise the breed."

"Then I shall just invite a few pretty girls to brighten up the party. Tell me who would please you—just someone to flirt with."

"Aren't *you* coming? Who else should be required to brighten any party you are attending, Maddie?" he asked, in a playful spirit.

She approved of his reply, as she approved of his scruples in dangling after herself, particularly when those scruples were possible of being overcome. She also approved of his next suggestion of going to the visitors' gallery at Westminster to listen in on a session of Parliament. When he was agreeable to accompany her to a rout party that same evening, she approved again.

"Come to dinner first," she invited. "There will be only Papa and myself and a few of his crones. I shan't invite Tilsit. It would look too contrived."

"No, don't invite him. I don't want to appear too anxious, or he won't offer me a good salary."

"Conniver!" she charged, but in a smiling way, still with approval.

She was perfectly happy with the world when her next caller was announced. It was Lord Eskott, who had not lessened his visits when he discovered it was four pence to a groat he would find Aldred with her, but did take less pleasure in them. Aldred took none at all.

"Is the boy not here holding your hand?" he asked in a sardonic voice.

"The boy has just left to audit a meeting at Westminster. I see he will not have the pleasure of hearing *you* speak. Why are you shirking your duty at this perilous time?"

"All work and no play, et cetera," he answered, taking up his customary seat beside her on the sofa before the grate.

"You have come to play with me, have you? How nice. What will it be: piquet, jackstraws?"

"Dutch uncle," he replied with a sapient look. "I am going to give you some unwelcome information with regard to your new boy."

"Meaning?" she asked, coming to sharp attention.

"I don't believe the fellow is playing straight with you, Maddie."

"I presume you have some basis for this extraordinary statement?"

"Yes, that old whore, Rumor, is my basis. Though shaky, it is one a lady seldom disregards. Rumor has it the boy is making inquiries with regard to employment within the ranks of the Whigs. He came to London with a letter in his pocket from his father, an ardent Whig, introducing him to Neville and some of the lesser lights amongst us. Of course he is not quite top drawer socially, and could hardly be expected to know the top dogs."

"Kind of you to describe my cousin as 'not quite top drawer,' Eskott. It is news to me if sons follow the politics of their fathers. It is the exception rather than the rule when they do."

"To be sure, I never took Aldred for an exceptional man in any way. Extremely common, I should say."

"You are at pains never to take him for a *man* at all, but always to describe him as a boy."

"*Your* boy is my customary term."

"Where did you hear this rumor? Have you spoken to Neville?"

"No, it would not be a rumor if I had. I confess I have the story second or third hand."

"What does rumor decree he has done about this letter? Has he been actively looking for a spot in your party?"

"He presented the letter to Neville. Neville, out of regard for his father, offered him the sort of minor post his lack of experience and acumen entitled him to. Aldred said neither yes nor no, but indicated he would think about it. For the past ten days he has been deeply cogitating the matter, while angling to see whether you haven't something better to offer. A plain old opportunist. He did not mention the matter to you, I take it?"

"Nothing. He knew I would dislike it."

"I should think you would like the secrecy even less."

"I do dislike it. I shall ask him about it."

"Be sure to tell him where you heard the rumor."

"You are at great pains to see he dislikes you!"

"I don't want the unpleasant chore of telling him *I* don't have a soft berth for him."

"I thought such a chore would be very much to your liking. Not that you're likely to have the pleasure of refusing him. Tilsit has just recently made him an excellent offer."

"Has he indeed? My worries were in vain

then. I am happy for you. What is the position to be?"

"It is not quite decided yet. He has to call on Tilsit to arrange the details."

"It is his intention to compare the offer to Neville's. You may lose him yet."

"He will accept some offer from Tilsit. The only uncertainty is whether he will become an M.P. through the courtesy of a seat belonging to Tilsit or act as secretary for him."

"There is nothing to prevent his doing both."

"I know that," she said angrily, though her anger was truly directed at her cousin for his lack of frankness with her.

"You don't have to snap my nose off!"

"I feel the need to snap off someone's. You happen to be here."

"It *does* bother you then, his duplicity?"

"It is not duplicity, only a lack of openness. Henry will have some explanation."

"I expect the boy is well versed in explaining away a lack of openness."

"The boy is twenty-four years old, only one year younger than myself."

"Strange, is it not? Twenty-four is young for a man, while twenty-five is *old* for a woman."

"Very strange indeed. One of the wonders of the physical world. Stranger yet when you take into consideration that women generally outlive their husbands by a decade or so. One would think women would choose husbands ten years younger than themselves."

"Perhaps they would, if they had the choosing, but that is a man's prerogative, like paying the bills. Am I to gather, as you introduced the comparison of your ages, that you are thinking in terms of making a match with the boy?"

"That subject again! What must I do to convince you, buy a herd of apes?"

"You give every appearance of being enamoured of him. Trotting with him four nights a week to routs and balls."

"You know I always show my protégés the ropes. It is a part of their initiation."

"How extremely tiring for you. Ratting on Aldred behind his back was only part of my reason for coming. I want to offer you a respite from your work. I am taking a party to Kent for the Christmas holiday. I would like you to join us. Your father, I know, will not like to come, but he is busier than usual this year, and will not miss you here. I have made it a non-political party, in your honor. No rampant politicos, but a nice heterogeneous blend of literati: Tom Moore has a young friend he wishes to bring along—chap named Byron. He has been abroad and has some verses he is about to publish on his travels. Some social lions and lionesses, a few sports-minded individuals, and of course a brace of dandies to entertain the ladies. Brummell has invited himself, and *I* am inviting *you.* Your Aunt Margaret is welcome to come along, if she likes. I have a ball planned to see in the new year, a few country dancing parties, skating on the pond if the cold weather holds up, but I hope it don't, skating notwithstanding."

It was a party designed to tempt her. For a minute she regretted her own party, already under preparation, the invitations not only out but accepted. It was clear that her wishes had been considered in the arranging of Eskott's do. "It sounds lovely, but we have already made plans for the holiday. We are off to Highgate."

"And you didn't invite *me,*" he said with mock offense. "Change your plans. There is time yet."

"No, it's too late. We go home for a week or ten days." As she compared her own dull party, comprised mostly of crones of her father, she wished she could cancel it.

"The boy goes with you?" he asked, a black brow lifting.

"Yes—that is, he has been invited." Oh dear, and if Henry did not come, after arranging the whole for him . . .

"What is the problem then? He will hardly refuse, when the thing was orchestrated with his career in mind, if I know anything."

"There is no problem. He will come. It is only that he had some thought of going home to visit his family, and must write his mama to tell her."

"I know nothing of his mother, but I warrant his father won't want him spending the holiday in the bosom of the enemy. I refer to political enemies, of course."

"I wonder if *that* is why he was reluctant," she said, really thinking aloud, though Eskott jumped on it at once.

"Oh ho, got yourself a reluctant boy this time, have you? That will be a change. Hardly a welcome one either."

"I admire his respect for the feelings of his family," she defended.

"No doubt, but the reluctance is less admirable, if I judge your scowl right. You definitely cannot come to me for the holiday then?"

"You can see it is impossible," she said, her disappointment lending a curt tone to her words.

"I'm sorry I went to the bother of arranging it then. That will teach me to count my guests before they're asked. I was really looking forward to a week's flirtation. Whom shall I ask instead? Lady Susan . . ." he began enumerating as he regarded her closely for reaction.

"Why not? She always seems an acceptable substitute—that is, an acceptable companion for you lately."

"She is the most agreeable *substitute* I have found yet. A substitute is never totally satisfactory though. I shall keep looking. I shan't wish you a merry Christmas yet. I expect we'll meet about here and there before we leave," he said, arising. "Any errands for me today? The wind is chill; you will not wish to go out."

"I am not a flower, Eskott. I don't mind a little breeze."

"Very well then, you ungrateful old weed. This is the thanks I get for looking out for your interest, and trying to entertain you. It makes it rather difficult for me to ask the favor that was my other reason for this visit. I was hoping to cadge your box at Drury Lane tonight. My Aunt Hilda and her dreary spouse are in town. Nothing will do them but Drury Lane, when I have chosen Covent Garden this year. Are you using your box?"

"No, take it by all means," she said, rising to fetch her ticket.

She was relieved, after he left, that there had been this amiable end to the visit, when the rest of it was so unpleasant. More unpleasant even than the prospect of missing his party was the unsettling news about Henry.

Chapter 6

There was no opportunity to quiz Henry about his application to Neville. He sent around a note that afternoon telling her he was going home at once. His mother was not well, and he was leaving that same day to visit her. This naturally made it impossible for him to attend her house party. He hoped she understood, and so on. She was feeling a trifle peaky herself, and did not go to the rout party she had planned to attend.

Eskott, not having seen her on the town, dropped around one morning to make his farewell before leaving for the country. "I have brought a small token of my esteem," he said, tossing her a book. "From the house guest I mentioned, Lord Byron. It won't be out till the new year, but I know you like to be in advance of all the vogues, and am lending you my review copy. It's rather good, if you care for that sensational sort of thing."

She glanced at the title, *Childe Harold,* before setting it aside. "Thank you, Eskott. Do sit down, if you're not in a great rush."

"To put so many miles between you and myself? Never. Oh, did I tell you I bumped into Hopper the other day? He was put out with you, milady," he said, waggling a finger at her.

"Hopper? Good gracious, I'm glad you jogged my memory. I wrote to the Admiralty about him. I meant to follow it up."

"Too late."

"Why? What has he done?"

"Switched jackets."

"He sold out his commission, the idiot. I told him not to."

"He did, but that was not the jacket I referred to."

"I had a post in mind for him."

"If the post you refer to is the sinecure at Plymouth, you left it too late. It's been taken."

"Who got it?"

"Some cousin or nephew of Lady Hertford. I don't recall the name. I *do* know, however, that there was no competition for the post. Quite sure you wrote that letter?"

"Of course I'm sure," she said, but even as she spoke, she had no real recollection of having *posted* the letter.

"Don't worry about Hopper. I got him something."

"You?" she asked with quick suspicion.

"Yes, I found him a bright, knowledgeable fellow. He's giving a hand to our party, a sort of scribbler for Rundell while waiting for a vacant seat to come up. We mean to put him into the Commons, where he can be heard."

"You're going to use him to speak against the Orders in Council!" she charged, her eyes sparkling dangerously. "That is poaching, Eskott! I didn't think you would be so low."

"He found the grazing lean in Tory preserves. I didn't think *you* would be slow in helping an erstwhile friend and favorite.

Neither did Hopper. The lad has no money to speak of. He needed work. You sat on your thumbs for a month, despite his repeated urgings. What was he to do? And in any case, what he has to say is too important for mere partisan feelings to enter into it. He is a gold mine of information, experience, on the curst Orders in Council."

"I'm tired of hearing about them. They are the law. They must be executed."

"No, the law must be changed. They are leading us inexorably into war with America. Quite apart from the morality of it, it is unthinkable to stretch our resources any thinner at this time, when we are contending with Napoleon."

"Napoleon issued his decrees first. What were we to do, let him sail all over us?"

"Some rational course could have been devised. It is irrational to expect the Americans to sit still while we board and search their ships, taking their men by force to serve on our own vessels. You may imagine how eager they are for the work. A great pleasure to their captains, I'm sure. It is no secret we have also licenced privateers to prey on American ships. At latest count, sixteen hundred American ships were lost in this way. Their export trade was cut to a quarter in one year. Whom are we trying to punish—the French or the Americans?"

"Whom are we trying to protect—the Americans or the English?"

"Ourselves, primarily. A stroke of genius on the government's part, robbing us of our needed raw products, and in turn robbing us of the lucrative American market for our manufactured goods. We'll never totally recover. The colonies are fast becoming self-sufficient. The Yanks have gone halfway, reducing their Embargo Act to the less stringent Non-intercourse Act. We ought to at least meet them halfway. It is madness to go on as we are. They might listen to a man like Hopper, who has first-hand experience."

"Did Hopper go to you, or did you go after him?"

"That's not important, Maddie. The culprit in the case is yourself. *You* didn't stir a finger to help him, after you *promised* you would. As a matter of fact, I looked the fellow up, planning only to pump him for anything I could learn about his experience. He mentioned he was *still* waiting to hear from you, after having written to jog your memory. He happened to mention the position he was waiting for. I checked with the Admiralty, and they had heard nothing from you. I went back and told him the position was taken, which it was. He was desolate, worried to death, with another child on the way and no roof over his head. It is unconscionable the way you have treated him. I think we both know what has deterred you from doing your duty."

"It's not *my* duty to find him a job."

"When you give him your word, it is your duty to carry it out."

"Well, don't bother dragging Henry into it. I was wrong, but it's not *his* fault."

"For once, your defense of him is just. I am happy you're man enough to admit it." He drew a deep sigh and continued: "I didn't want this last visit to be so unpleasant. I don't know why I feel *I* must be your conscience, except that your father doesn't perform that duty very satisfactorily."

"Never mind. Lady Susan will soon cheer you up. She has agreed to accompany you home for the holiday, I trust?"

"She has. In fact, we are leaving this afternoon. I'm driving her and her mother. An eye for an eye, you know. You will have your Henry with you at Highgate, and I my Susan."

"Henry is not coming after all." He looked at her, his interest quickening. "In fact, I am fed up with Henry," she admitted, annoyance with her own laxness over Hopper, regret at having to miss Eskott's party, and some little jealousy of Lady Susan all coalescing into a fit of pique. "Why don't you stay and take luncheon with me before you go? I shall be all alone. Papa is not coming home. Cheer me up, dear Eskott," she said, reaching her hand out to him.

He grabbed it swiftly and squeezed her fingers. "Today you will take into your head to be civil, when I have asked guests home to lunch."

"Lady Susan?" she asked.

"Yes."

"Be sure to give her my best wishes for the holiday. In that way, she will know you came to say good-bye to me," she added with an arch smile. "Also my very best to yourself, of course."

"Still friends, despite all my badgering?" he asked.

"The best friend I have in the world. But no more poaching, if you please."

He looked at her for a long minute in silence, with an expression that was difficult to read. There was admiration in it, and some less happy emotion. "I wish you were coming with us," he said.

"I wish I were too," she answered with a wistful frown.

"Maddie!" He lunged forward, pulling her into his arms. There was a wild look of hope in his startled eyes. "Do you mean it?"

"Certainly I do. I always loved Bleumont. We have had such good times there."

"Make it yours too, permanently. You know I've always loved you." She made some little effort to push him away, but he was determined to finish what he had started, and held her tightly, fixing his lips against hers till she stopped struggling and even enjoyed the unexpected embrace. Eskott was damnably attractive, and she was not a young girl, abashed at passion. She felt some satisfaction at what Lady Susan would think, if she could see them at this moment. When at length he stopped, a slow and happy smile stole over his harsh features.

"Miss Morash, I ask you for the second and last time, will you marry me? Oh Maddie, do! We could be so happy . . ."

"Eskott, you ninnyhammer!" she exclaimed, laughing. "You're mature enough to know one swallow doesn't make a spring, and one kiss doesn't make a lady a bride either. I don't want to get married yet."

"*Yet?* It's been *years!* You're getting on, Maddie, and so am I. How long must I wait?"

"I didn't mean . . . It's not a matter of *time,* dear heart. You and I will never be more than good friends, but *do* let us continue friends. There is no one I esteem more. *Please?*" she asked, smiling sweetly. Then on an inspiration, she reached over and placed a maidenly kiss on his cheek. "I shan't tell Susan, if you don't tell Henry. Agreed?"

"I am not accountable to Lady Susan for my actions. I understood you were through with Henry too," he said, his voice harsh.

"Fed up, not through. I'm just disappointed he is not coming to Highgate with us for the holiday."

To save face, Eskott gave her no argument. He pulled out his watch, though there was a clock not four feet away from him on the mantel. "I really must be off.

Give my best wishes to your father and Lady Margaret."

"We'll see you after the holiday?" she asked.

"Very likely. I hardly ever die of disappointment. Good day."

He bowed and left rather quickly, feeling like a fool and a badly disappointed one too. Madeline smiled idly. It was very satisfying to know that Eskott still loved her. She could hardly be considered over the hill, when the most eligible bachelor in town was dancing at her skirts. Oh dear, and she had meant to send a nice note to that Byron fellow, praising his poems, though she had not actually found time to read them.

She was busy, with her own trip to arrange. It was necessary to write a few notes begging off city parties. While at this chore, she found the unposted note to Dundas, and felt a twinge of guilt. She knew she ought to pen a message to Hopper explaining, but really there was no explanation to give; and besides, he had turned coat on her and deserved no apology. She went upstairs to give her dresser instructions for packing. There was a small dinner party at her own home that evening, over early, to allow a good night's rest before an early start for Highgate in the morning.

The Christmas party was strangely unsatisfying to Madeline. She was unsure whether it was due to the knowledge she was missing out on a livelier do at Eskott's place, or to Aldred's absence. The days were short. Already by four or four-thirty the skies darkened, indicating another long evening to be got in. She sat around a roaring fire listening to a bunch of elderly politicians discuss their world, realization slowly but surely dawning on her that her real interest in it all was not the running of the country's affairs but her own running of one particular young man. If Henry were there to put forward, to make shine in front of the two ministers and several other influential gentlemen, she would be well entertained. She wrested what pleasure she could from visiting old country friends; from one skating party, for the weather remained cold; and from one country assembly. But on the whole she was just plain bored.

She was giving serious consideration to curtailing the party, to returning to the city in time for the new year. Perhaps Henry would be there. She would have a party.

That she and her father already had a party planned at Highgate was not so much forgotten as ignored. Then she received a letter from Henry, which changed the mood of depression that was settling over her. It was brief, but contained good news. His mother had recovered—it was not so serious a cold as he feared. Might he present himself at this late date for the tail end of her party? It was a rhetorical question. He was already on his way, to arrive that same afternoon.

How brightly the sun was suddenly shining! It gleamed an iridescent orange, gold, and green on the new-fallen snow. Her own new year's party suddenly seemed an excellent idea after all. It would be enlarged, more youngsters invited to give it a livelier air. The old men around the fire were listened to with a keener ear, now that there was a specific purpose to understanding their chatter.

It was on that day she acknowledged to herself that she had fallen in love at last. She was in love with Henry Aldred. She had always supposed that when love came, and she had not actually despaired of its coming, despite her allegations to the contrary, it would be some highly placed, worldly, older man who would win her. That it would be a provincial fellow younger than herself, and a good deal less versed in the doings of the world, was a fascination to her. It was true love then, the head-spinning, heart-lifting, oblivious-to-the-rest-of-the-world sort of a passion she had been waiting for. Henry had not yet made his mark, but with her behind him, doors would open swiftly. Money would no longer be a problem. They could live with Papa for the present, saving up her income to buy a place of their own when Lord Fordwich died and his heir took over the estates. By then Henry would be established too, making a worthwhile salary of his own. All this was settled in her mind before ever he arrived.

She knew as soon as he came in that the absence had worked the same miracle on him. He looked at her with a brighter, more proprietary eye. His conversation was more personal, more closely verging on the lover-like.

"How nice to see you again!" was his first speech, when she met him at the door. He seized her two hands in his cold fingers. After an awkward moment, he bent down and placed a cousinly kiss on her cheek.

"There, that is for looking so beautiful," he said with a shy smile, as though conscious that he imposed on her good humor. "Even better than I have been dreaming . . . *remembering,*" he adjusted quickly. She drew him into the hallway, still holding on to his hand, to see her Aunt Margaret coming forward.

Her aunt was a comfortable middle-aged matron. Lady Margaret preferred the ease of country life to the bustle of the city. She had no keen interest in fashion. Her gowns were dark and simple, her hair unstyled, her figure unbound by a corset. She had achieved a roly-poly shape, and a wide, round face, whose main charm was its good-humored smile.

"So you're the young man I've been hearing so much about," she said, running a practiced eye over him. A modish many-collared greatcoat hid his jacket, but even without a view of Weston's work, it was clear to her that Maddie had found herself a very handsome one this season.

Madeline made the introductions. "Your niece has been holding out on me," Henry said. "She hasn't told me a thing about *you,* but Papa tells me he has the honor of your acquaintance, ma'am."

"I knew him when he was in shortcoats. I suppose he has got over that nasty habit of thrusting toads and frogs into a girl's face by this time?"

"I believe so. Now that he is more mature, he thrusts badgers and rats. He most particularly asked me to inquire whether *you* still hide your head under a pillow at night to escape the bogeyman who used to visit you when the moon was full."

"No, I still do it," she said with a laugh. "Imagine Andy remembering that. We spent a summer together once about a hundred or so years ago, on a farm in Scotland. I can't recall how it came about. My mama was in the straw, but I don't know what accounted for Andy's visit."

"I expect my papa was in the basket," he answered lightly.

"I'll have the butler show you to your room, Henry," Madeline said, eager to get him to herself. "Come to the study when you are freshened up. We have such a lot to talk about."

"I like him," Lady Margaret said when he had gone abovestairs. "A handsome fellow, I always liked Andrew Aldred. He would have amounted to something in the world if he had made a decent marriage.

It would be a pity if his sons followed in his footsteps. I expect their papa has cautioned them against such a course. I suppose you have a well-dowered young girl all picked out for him by this time, eh Maddie?"

"It's a bit early for that yet," Madeline answered blandly, but a blush betrayed her feelings.

"I do not refer to yourself, goose. You can look higher than Mr. Aldred. Still, he is a bright, lively lad. It will be nice to have some young company in the house for you."

Within minutes, Henry was back downstairs, searching Madeline out in the study. She ordered tea and a sandwich for him, then sat down to talk.

"Before we begin, Madeline, I have some confessions to make," he said, casting his brown eyes on her in a beseeching way.

"What is it?" she demanded, alarmed, with some premonition that it involved a girl.

"About my foot-dragging in the matter of Tilsit's offer. The fact is, when I went to London, I was instructed by my father to go to Neville, a friend of his. I don't know whether the name means anything to you, but he is a Whig. He offered me a position, a paltry job really, but that is not why I refused it. At the moment, I don't merit anything better than that. I refused because you had convinced me my interests lay elsewhere. I knew my welcome at your home would be removed if I accepted Neville, and how could I deprive myself of my only joy in London? But till I talked it over with my father, explained my reasons to him in person, I disliked to definitely turn Neville down. It would have hurt my father, had he heard the news from Neville and not me. That was the real reason I went home, to unencumber myself of my guilty secret to Papa. He was understanding, however. Once he learned I truly believed in the principles of the Tories, he urged me to put my efforts where my feelings were. He's a wonderful man, my father. I wish you could meet him. Now that I have convinced him, I can give Tilsit his reply. I shall see him as soon as we get to London."

"I don't see why you could not have told me all this sooner," she objected. "But it is no matter. I am satisfied with it. It is unusual to find a young man who takes such consideration of his parents' wishes nowadays. I respect you for it, Henry. And your mother . . . ?"

"She had a cold. I would not *lie* outright about it. It was not very serious. She is all recovered, thank God. You are so understanding, Cousin. I hope you will not lose your respect for me when you hear the rest. *Some* confessions, I said. The fact is, I was—now how shall I say it?—entangled with a girl at home. Not serious, you know, but when you have been on good and friendly terms with a young lady for a year, some private conversation is necessary to let her know nothing is going to come of it. We were not committed in any way, no engagement, nothing of that sort. It is only that she might have had some expectations. You know how silly some girls are. You stand up with them twice, and they take the notion an offer is about to be made. We parted on the best of terms, no hearts broken, no hard feelings on either side. In fact, I come to think I was overly solicitous for her feelings. She already had another fellow on the string, but when you deal with people's *feelings*, you don't want to risk hurting them. There, that is my last confession for the day. Are you wretchedly disappointed in me? I have been unattractively secretive in my dealings with you. I want that to be all over between us. You know exactly where I stand. My heart is lighter for having told you."

"Wretch! To get me all in a dither for nothing. I'm sure there are dozens of girls brokenhearted to see you leave your home. If the chit you speak of has got herself another beau already, she cannot have been brokenhearted."

"No, and neither am I. She seemed so terribly rustic, so narrow in her interests to me after being with you—in the city, I mean, mixing with all the people you have introduced me to. Quite spoiled me for the provincial life. You had better make me a prime minister, milady, for you have ruined me for the station to which I was born."

"Who is to say you were born to molder in the country? There is nothing to stand in the way of anyone's getting to the top. It is not only in America that men are born equal."

"Money, for one thing, stands in the way. The lack of it, I mean."

"If that is all that's keeping you out of the prime minister's seat, we must find you a nice, rich wife," she suggested, regarding him closely, but in a careful way, pretending to glance past his head out the window.

"Have you anyone special in mind?" he asked softly.

"No, how should I so soon? Give me the commission, and I shall present half a dozen debs for your perusal, sir."

"Don't limit the selection to *debs*, Maddie. I always preferred older ladies." His eyes were smiling, admiring, questioning, bright with interest.

"What would a young rogue like you want with an older lady?" she quizzed.

"I don't mean ancient. No gray-haired widows, if you please. Some lady with town bronze, to guide me through the shoals and narrows of the wicked city. Any friend of yours . . ."

"The ladies who made their bows with me are mostly married, unless they are positive antidotes. I don't suppose you would settle for a squint, or a gapped-tooth smile?"

"I am convinced you will find me someone. I leave the matter entirely in your capable hands. If you fail, then I have an idea myself . . ."

No more was said on the subject, but

the look they exchanged expressed a complete understanding.

"I'm very glad you told me everything. The fact is, Eskott came running to me with tales of your speaking to Neville, and of course I was furious."

"You must have been ready to boil me in oil. I might have known Eskott would do me a bad turn if he could. He's in love with you, isn't he?"

"He is fond of me. We're very old friends."

"He's in love with you. But I know you don't lead him on. He is seen everywhere recently with Lady Susan Someone-or-other. A plain-looking girl, and old as the hills."

Madeline knew the lady was younger than herself, but she said nothing of that. "He is more often seen at the Second Court of St. James, I believe."

The end of the holiday passed like a sort of magical dream. She was seldom away from Henry. They drove, walked, and skated together during the day. In the evenings, they went to one country do, and on two occasions had guests in to be entertained. Henry was gallant, attentive, jealous of any competition, with a blend of subservience, awareness of his inferior position, yet manly firmness that could not but please her. During any spare hours, they talked with the older men, hearing more than once that Perceval was all that put their government in jeopardy.

"It's a crying shame Perceval won't step aside, for the good of the party, and let you take over in his stead," Henry said indignantly, aiming his flattery in Fordwich's direction.

The old man was in perfect agreement with him. He could not suggest such a thing himself, but was grateful to hear it said.

When Henry went on to butter up each minister in his turn, he was soon found to be a "bright young lad" and a "comer." The party needed more like him. The approval of Henry was almost palpable in the room.

For the last few days of the party, Madeline seldom gave a thought to Eskott's gala do, proceeding at a lively pace without her. Her party for the new year was enlarged to ball-like proportions, though it was not called a ball. Henry looked devastatingly handsome in his black outfit, with a shirt as white as snow displayed at his neck. The country gentlemen faded into insignificance beside him. All her old friends were gazing in admiration, whispering that Lady Madeline was to make a match at last. Madeline outdid herself in the matter of toilette. She chose white, which brought Aunt Margaret's wrath down on her head.

"Back to your debutante days, are you, Maddie? I like you better in colors. It don't make you look a day younger to deck yourself out like a young girl."

"I'm only twenty-five, Auntie. Not quite hagged yet, do you think?"

"More importantly, Mr. Aldred don't seem to think so. Your papa will never allow a match, Maddie. Oh, I know you are going to tell me he hasn't offered, but he will. You are giving him more than enough encouragement. It isn't right to lead the fellow on, only to have to turn him down in the end. It isn't like you to be so thoughtless."

"Who says I will turn him down?" Madeline answered sharply.

"*I* say your father will turn him off. It is all well and good to amuse yourself by playing puppet mistress with your boys, but this goes beyond the others. I don't like it. And furthermore, I come to think I don't like Mr. Aldred as well as I did. I heard him being very toplofty with the Smileys last night. There is no reason for him to be looking down his nose at them. They could buy and sell him."

"Very likely, but they cannot touch him for intelligence."

"Sly, I call it, to be sitting listening to the old fellows talk, then parroting their own thoughts back at them, to get their approval. I haven't heard anything in the way of an original idea come out of his handsome mouth."

"He has to make his way in the world. He won't do it by arguing with the men in power. He is young; naturally he must listen and learn."

"Must he also toady up to them? 'Let me get you a glass of port, sir.' 'Have you seen this article in the *Herald,* Lord Timmins?' 'How I should love to be able to sit in on one of the cabinet meetings, and hear you all speak.' Little better than toad-eating, if you ask *me.*"

"I don't recall asking you, Auntie."

"I'm telling you all the same, and I'll tell you something else you won't like, miss. I'm going back to London with you, to see you don't make a complete fool of yourself. I don't know why you couldn't marry someone of our own sort, like Eskott."

"Eskott may go to the devil!"

"He'll find Aldred there, if he does," Lady Margaret declared with great feeling before she strode from the room. Though her face was red and her talk loud, she was more worried than angry. She was old and wise enough to have seen these wild infatuations before; to know they did not last long, but were violent and dangerous while the fever raged. She had lived with her brother, Fordwich, forever, helping his wife raise Madeline. She loved the girl as her own daughter, but had not a mother's authority. Fordwich was no help. He was so wrapped up in this business of the regent's turning out the government that he never saw a thing that went on in his own home. He had seen enough men come and go in Madeline's favor that he paid little heed to her flirtations.

The little scold fell on deaf ears. It had already been forgotten when Madeline descended the grand staircase moments later to see Henry waiting for her below, his face turned up to watch her approach. "Exquisite!" was all he said. The tone of his voice caressing; the touch of the fingers, with just a little intimate pressure; the eyes glowing with pride and possession—they were enough to turn a cynic's head, and Madeline was not yet hardened into a cynic. There was a joyous agitation amounting almost to a pain in her chest. She knew in some intuitive way that she would never forget this moment. There was a bustle of activity behind Henry, of guests arriving to sit down to dinner before the ball. A cold draught blew in from the open doorway. She was dimly aware of this without having to look, or feel, or listen. All her conscious attention was riveted on Henry, and her own heart. She gazed at him for a long moment, then smiled.

"I—I must welcome the guests," she said. Her voice was breathless.

"Of course." He stood readily aside to allow her to pass. She knew he was looking after her.

They were not seated at all close to each other at dinner—Aunt Margaret's work, Maddie thought, with a twinge of annoyance. No matter, soon they would be together. Tonight he would stifle all his scruples and speak, offer for her. There was not a doubt in her mind. He would ask her to marry him, and she would accept. There would be one loud, long terrible brouhaha with Auntie and Papa, and then it would be over. They would give in, in the end. They always did. You could get nearly anything you wanted, if you held firm. Madeline had learned this lesson while still in short dresses and long hair. All you really needed to get what you wanted was conviction, for there was very little of it abroad in the world. Most folks were reeds in the wind, waiting for a breeze of conviction to come along and bend them.

Lady Madeline was perfectly charming to all her guests that evening. She performed country dances with neighboring solicitors and parsons, the minuet with tired members of Parliament, but she saved the one waltz for Henry. It was this new dance's first introduction into her part of the countryside. Only three couples performed, while all the others looked on, staring at such wanton debauchery being performed in public, eagerly trying to learn the steps that they might try it at the next assembly. She floated around the floor in Henry's arms, too happy to speak. As the music ended, they spun near a doorway that led to the rear portion of the hall. They exchanged a speaking glance, and went out to find some privacy.

"We can talk in here," Madeline said, opening the door into a small parlor in common use as her aunt's sewing room.

Henry closed the door behind them. "Talk? I have gone beyond talking, Maddie," he said, his voice a husky whisper, as he drew her into his arms for a passionate embrace. She had been kissed before, by a round half-dozen gentlemen. None of them had caused this ecstatic turmoil she now experienced. The kiss began with a gentle touching of the lips, that kindled to a frenzy, then gradually subsided to a lingering warmth that left her weak.

"Forgive me! Forgive me, darling," he murmured in her ear.

"Never—unless you ask me to marry you at once," she said, clinging to him.

"I am in no position to. I shouldn't have allowed myself the luxury around . . . who could resist you? You know my situation, Maddie. What a wretched match it would be for you."

"Any other match would be *unthinkable,* after this," she told him.

He folded her in his arms, tightly against his chest, with her cheek resting on his shoulder. "One day, one day *soon* I hope, I will have the right to offer for you," he said in ardent accents. Then he strove to change his tone. "Do you think you can wait for me, my darling?"

"For a little while," she answered, matching her mood to his. "But I must warn you, sir, I am not at all a patient lady. I expect to see you prime minister by the end of this new year."

"Agreed!" he said at once. "We shall be married one year from today, if I am prime minister. Now we must get back to our—*your* guests. You see I already consider myself an adjunct to you."

He released her, just holding on to one hand in a painfully firm grip. She smiled triumphantly. The year, she felt, would soon dwindle into six months. For herself, she had no notion of waiting more than half a year. A June wedding would be nice.

"Have you spoken to Papa yet?" she asked.

"No, I had intended to keep a guard on my tongue tonight, but your beauty slipped past it. I couldn't control myself. I must speak to him soon, but we shan't spoil this perfect holiday with any scenes. After I am settled into something in London will be time enough. Will he be violently angry with me?"

"No, with *me,* but I can always handle him."

Chapter 7

Lady Margaret stuck by her decision to return to London with the family. Her concern for her niece mounted high enough that she cautioned her brother to speak to his daughter.

"Nonsense, Meggie," he scoffed, "Maddie always runs around with her new protégé every year. It is her way of amusing herself. Don't go putting ideas into her head. She'll not marry *him.* He has not spoken to me about such a thing. I will be sure to hint him away if he does. My cousin's son after all; I cannot be rude to him with no cause."

"You don't have to be rude to *him.* Tell Maddie she is making a cake of herself," was the rejoinder. "She follows him around like a mother hen at all the parties, putting on such a display of owning him it has got all the old cats talking."

Fordwich took it for a spinster's imaginings. It was perfectly clear to him that his daughter's only interest in the fellow was his career. She always put him forward when a chance presented itself. She had counseled him not to accept Tilsit's offer after all, as it was beneath him. Fordwich was rather inclined to agree with her. Very sound judgment the young man had in talking up Perceval's retirement. Pity the lad wasn't in a position to hint the same to Perceval, for it was proving a demmed hard thing for any of the others to do, and his obstinacy was all that left the Tory tenure hanging in the balance. The present thinking was that Wellesley, the foreign secretary, would prove an entirely suitable replacement for Perceval. That Henry hinted to Fordwich the proper replacement resided at St. James's Street did nothing to lessen the father's evaluation of the youngster's intelligence.

"I am too old," he said sadly. "Wellesley is our man. He means to tender his resignation as foreign secretary to leave himself open for the promotion. He will cite Perceval's lack of vigor in pursuing the Peninsula campaign as his reason. It is well known the regent is in favor of it. He'll not take the resignation of Wellington's brother sitting down. It is Perceval who will go; then we are in power to stay. Perceval can hardly refuse to take the prince's suggestion. Come February, it will be more than a suggestion too."

Madeline, alert to her lover's future, arranged that Henry be present at a dinner party to which she also invited Wellesley. "If you are to be secretary to anyone, it might as well be the prime minister himself," she pointed out. "It will be easier to accomplish *before* he becomes the new chief."

"What if his resignation is accepted, and he is *not* made prime minister?" Henry countered. "Then I am out in the wilderness of the back benches. Of course, if I could get the offer and delay my acceptance till he is promoted . . ."

"It won't be accomplished in a day, Henry," she warned. "You can hardly keep him dangling a month."

"He hasn't offered yet," he replied, frowning in concentration.

"I shouldn't be at all surprised if he broaches the matter this evening. He has some little inkling that Papa's support involves your appointment. It was not put into such blunt words, of course, but Wellesley is subtle enough to read between the lines, I think. He is no stranger to nepotism."

Madeline, the busy diplomat, was at pains to outline her cousin's interest and preference for a prime minister to Wellesley that same evening.

"Congratulations, sir," was Henry's salutation to the foreign secretary. "It is an honor to shake the hand of our next prime minister."

"Oh as to that . . ." Wellesley disavowed, restraining any outward show of joy, "there is no saying what will come of it. It is a matter of conscience with me that I will not serve under Perceval, but that is not to say I expect to replace him."

"You must not disappoint us, sir," Henry replied. "The country expects it of you."

"My family has never been reluctant to do its duty," Wellesley answered modestly.

"Indeed it has not! The name has been carried to all points of the globe—India, the Peninsula, where your brother is now distinguishing himself, and his country."

There was some discussion of the Peninsular campaign, after which Wellesley, well impressed with Fordwich's cousin, asked, "Just what is your official capacity at the moment, Mr. Aldred? I keep seeing you about here and there, hear everyone speak of you, but I don't believe I have heard exactly who it is you are working for."

"I have been considering various offers. I just recently came up to London. Lord Tilsit wants me to take a northern seat or work for him, but I am not at all sure the price of corn is my chief concern at this moment."

"It is an important matter at any time, but hardly the most *exciting* matter on the books. Your broad general interest and knowledge might be better used in a different capacity."

This "broad interest" was felt by both Henry and Madeline to refer to the speaker's pending position as prime minister. "I have been busying myself to get a grasp of the overall picture," Henry replied at once.

"That's very interesting. Very interesting. We too seldom see such a breadth of vision in the young. We shall be speaking again soon, I expect. Ah, there is Sidmouth. I must say good evening to him."

Henry looked with a bemused smile at Wellesley's departing form. A prime minister-to-be, speaking to an ex-prime minister, and both of them on terms with himself. How his world had widened since he'd come to London! Both he and Madeline felt that if the post as Wellesley's assistant had not actually been offered, it was certainly in the offing.

And indeed it was. The hoped-for offer was made three days later. By then it was known that Wellesley's resignation had not been accepted. He was no longer being touted as Perceval's replacement, and his offer was politely declined.

"You don't mean you *refused* him?" Madeline asked when Henry told her the tale. "He is still a very influential man, Henry. The foreign secretary—it's an enormously important post, and his secretary would be much noticed too."

"How long will he continue as foreign secretary?" Henry countered. "It seems to me this was Prinney's chance to dump Perceval, if that is all that troubles him about his government. Why did he not do it? This was his chance, but he didn't take it. No, Maddie, I think the old boys who sit stroking their chins about your fire are badly mistaken about their chances for holding on to power. They are on their way out the door, and are too stupid—that is, blinded by prejudice—to see it."

"What if they *do* have a few terms out

of office? It's not the end of the world. No government is in power forever. You work in opposition, work as hard as you can, then when the Tories are back in the saddle, you are given a prime post. That's the way politics works, Henry."

"Yes, but why should I hitch my wagon to a dead horse? If the Whigs are to form a government—"

"I doubt very much that they will," she interrupted.

"Now don't be angry with me. You *know* why I am so impatient to get on with making a name for myself. One year is all I have to reach the top of the heap, remember? I dare not make a wrong step."

"But really, my dear, you must make *some* step. You cannot go on claiming to have just arrived in town forever. Your face is becoming too familiar for that."

"I am desperately short of funds," he admitted, disconsolate. "I dislike to ask my father for more. He has a large family to provide for, you know. If only I could find something to tide me over for a few weeks."

"Something non-political, do you mean?"

"Yes, but pray do not suggest I set up as someone's tutor. It's ridiculous really—

your father working so hard, and he an old man, and here am I, young and robust, and unable to find anything to do."

"Yes, Papa is feeling the result of all the worry and scheming that has been going on."

"I wish I could help him in some way."

"It would bring you closer to him, make him realize how worthwhile you really are. Henry . . ."

Before the sun set, Henry was established as Lord Fordwich's unofficial helper. He worked out of the house on St. James's Square, which delighted Madeline. At any hour of the day, she had only to open her father's study door to find him. He was paid enough to cover his daily expenses, and in return performed those routine chores that could lighten Fordwich's burden and, in theory, instruct the young man in the art of government. Everyone was pleased with the arrangement except Lady Margaret, who took to slamming doors and sniping at everyone who came near her.

Eskott did not discontinue his visits, despite the second rejection of his offer of marriage. He came shortly after the new year to crow over the success of his house party.

"You should have been there, Maddie. You would have had an inner track with the new beau of London. Byron was a tremendous hit. A walking Apollo, and a demmed talented one too. The ladies are all running mad for him."

"He gave you some stiff competition, did he?" she asked, undismayed. Such matters as new peers of talent and beauty usually excited sharp interest from her. Eskott was curious to notice her lack of concern. "How did your do go?" he asked.

"Fine, very nice. No lavish balls nor anything of that sort. A quiet party."

"I expect you were dull as ditch water, without the boy there."

"Henry did manage to come to us for the latter part of the holiday," she informed him with a satisfied smile.

"Did he indeed? The mama recovered then, I assume?"

"Yes, she did."

"I hope the young lady he jilted at home did likewise," he told her with a sapient look.

Madeline snapped to attention. "More scandal-mongering behind his back? What did you do, send spies along to check up on him, Eskott?"

"No, I am not so interested as all that. Merely I have friends from the vicinity who were home for the holidays. They tell me he broke off with some young heiress he was dangling after before he came to London."

"It is not news to me. If I had known you were so interested in my cousin, I could have told you all about it. He *did* terminate an old affair with an erstwhile lady friend while he was home. Terminated it to their mutual satisfaction, I might add. There was nothing in the nature of a jilting, unless her having taken up with another beau might be called jilting Henry."

"We must allow it to be inconceivable that any lady of sound mind would jilt Henry," he replied mockingly. He had to accept her version of the story. She was acquainted with one of the principals, while he had his story second hand, and then only after a good deal of trouble in tracking down anyone from the vicinity of Manchester who knew of the affair. It was difficult for a proud man to be pestering friends for this sort of sordid scandal.

"What had he to say of my other piece of backbiting, the affair of the letter to Neville?"

"He admitted it. He spoke to Neville out of respect for his father, and declined the offer out of respect for common sense."

"Have you found him a more—er, *sensible* position? You will notice, I hope, that I never suggest the paragon go out and find something for himself."

"Yes, I am aware of all your little barbs, Eskott. Henry has had many interesting offers."

"Which of them has he accepted?"

"None. He is presently lending Papa a hand. He is extremely busy at this time, you know. It is a temporary thing only."

"Planning to rig him out in the family livery?"

"If he joins the family, it will not be as a liveried servant, but as something quite different," she replied, her good humor causing Eskott to regard her with the utmost suspicion.

He looked for one long, incredulous moment, then threw his head back and laughed. "You ain't such a grudgeon as that, Maddie, to go hitching yourself to a provincial nobody, who must batten himself on your father. He has neither position, influence, money, nor even sufficient age to attract you."

"I never had any preference for white hair, actually. *Boys,* you recall, were always my weakness."

"You are sensible enough to have a preference for something other than a fortune hunter, I hope?"

"Oh yes, I am not slow to turn off all fortune hunters who cross my path."

"You will be giving him his congé soon then, I expect."

"Did you come here for the sole purpose of being disagreeable, Eskott? How thoughtful of you. You have done your duty now, and may leave with the knowledge that I am very angry with you."

"I notice the green eyes are shooting emerald sparks. I have scored a hit, whether you acknowledge it or not. But annoying you was not my only reason for coming. I also want to crow a little. Wellesley's bid for the P.M.'s job was turned down flat. Looks as if Prinney is planning to dump the Tories after all, eh?"

"Don't hold your breath waiting. A man could suffocate that way. There isn't more than a handful of you Whigs he wants—yourself, I might add, not amongst them. If he can't get the chosen few under Tory leadership, he won't bother with any of you at all. He will have done his token duty, and will settle down with the old boys for another millennium or so."

"Ah yes, the gospel according to Saint Perceval," he said, striking his breast and lowering his head, as though at vespers. "Let me clue you in on the Brougham version. The Tories have all the power, while the Whigs have all the talent. It is only the prince's monumental stupidity that holds the country back. Of course when a man takes counsel from a lady, what is to be expected? I refer of course to the Old Lady of Manchester Square. Still, I expect your version is accurate, if more savage and cynical than one might expect from a female. The *gentler* sex, we besotted males consider you. I really don't know why. From Eve down to the present, you are always eager to outwit and betray us."

"And it is so easy to do, too!" she said, smiling.

While they were still talking, Henry Aldred arrived from having picked up some folders at Westminster. "Good afternoon, Eskott," he said pleasantly, after first making a bow to Madeline. "Your father wants me to bring him some documents he left at home, but he shan't need them till this evening. It looks like another night session coming up. I plan to answer these few letters for him before I go back."

"Can you stay for dinner?" she asked, a smile of pleasure lighting her face.

"I must be back by eight. If we eat early . . . But you are dining with the Earls this evening, are you not?"

"I'll cancel that," she said.

Eskott looked at her, dumbfounded. His little worries that she was beginning to take a more serious than usual interest in her new protégé were suddenly seen to be out of date. She was infatuated with him. The beaming smile that she could not hold in, the willingness to change her plans for him, the very air around the pair spoke of love. What the haughty beauty could see in the jackanapes was past imagining. A well-shaped head and a well-cut jacket—these were his advantages. She was no young, inexperienced girl either, but a lady who had been on the town long enough to know better. But she looked like a young girl today. A young, radiant girl, very much in love.

"Can't you sit down and join us for a moment, Aldred?" Eskott invited, noticing from the corner of his eye Maddie's annoyance. She wanted him to leave, to get her lover to herself.

"I am always happy to meet the opposition," Henry said lightly, taking up a seat. "I expect there is a deal of disenchantment in your camp these days."

"Because of the delay in bringing the Whigs into power, you mean?" Eskott asked, surprised, or giving a good simulation of it.

"Delay? He doesn't mean to bring you into power at all."

"Is *that* the nonsense they have been feeding you here at the Second Court of St. James? Wait till February, when the restrictions on his powers expire. He'll have your set out so fast your heads will spin. I cannot imagine why any young man who wishes to get ahead would throw in his lot with the wrong party, especially when his relations have long been Whigs. Neville was very disappointed at your refusing his offer. He had big things in mind for you."

Aldred looked interested, but with Madeline at his side he said the necessary things. "We'll hold, Eskott," he finished, after a little repetition of the Tory gospel.

Eskott laughed and shrugged his shoulders. "Time will tell whether you have not made a grave error. I only know Brougham has had the windows at Ten Downing Street measured for blue drapes, and ordered a new mattress to the bed, for he says he will not lie down in a Tory manger."

"He's roasting you, Henry," Madeline explained. "Pay no heed to Eskott. He only came to annoy me. He has already confessed as much. And you have annoyed me quite enough for one day, milord."

"Very well then, I shall behave, but I think it an abominable stunt you are playing on your cousin, leading him astray in this manner. They must be hiding all the more secret documents from you, Henry. Of course the Tories are famous for hiding the truth."

"Is this your notion of behaving?" Madeline inquired.

"My last outburst. I know when I am not wanted. Do you go to Sidmouth's ball this evening, Maddie?"

"How late will you be working, Henry?" she asked, before giving him her answer.

"Till nine-thirty or ten."

"Then you will be finished in time to take me. You may look to the doorway around ten-thirty to see us making our grand entrance, Eskott. You are attending, I take it?"

"Certainly I'll be there."

"You could go with Lady Margaret, if you don't want to wait so late for me," Henry mentioned.

"What, is Meggie in town?" Eskott asked.

"Yes, she returned with us after the holiday. I really cannot imagine why. She doesn't *go* anywhere, but only stomps up and down halls and stairs, rattling the china and frowning at everyone."

"I would like to say good day to her."

"I think I hear her banging around now. Either that or we are being visited by an earthquake. I'll call her."

When she left the room, Henry said, "I must get busy if I am to be finished with this work for Fordwich. But before I go— Neville was disappointed with my refusal, was he?"

"Very much so. We all were, but you are comfortably ensconced in another nest now, and it wouldn't do for me to be poaching. Maddie has already rung a peel over me on that score."

"I am only helping my cousin, Fordwich, with a little of his correspondence. It's as much personal estate business as anything else, to leave him free for politics. He's so busy, it is the least I can do."

"I think it a great waste of your time and talents to be nothing more than a scribbler, but then I'm sure you know what you are about," Eskott said, biting back a sharper rejoinder. Estate business was not conducted from Westminster.

"My cousins have been so kind to me, you know, that I could hardly refuse to give Fordwich a hand when he asked."

"Yes, I quite understand your position."

Lady Margaret entered smiling. Henry left, and as Madeline did not return to the saloon, Eskott assumed she had joined her cousin in her father's study.

"I haven't seen you in two years, Eskott. I hope you're keeping well? Have you time to join me for a cup of tea? Nasty cold weather we are having."

"That would be nice. I had not heard you were in town or I would have been here sooner to pay my respects."

"I hadn't intended coming, but . . ." She stopped, with a worried glance to the doorway.

"Is it Aldred that has you worried?"

"Aldred and that foolish niece of mine.

She is infatuated with him, Eskott. There is no other word for it."

"Surely Fordwich does not go along with it?"

"He refuses to see what is going on beneath his nose. I *don't* understand it, unless it is Aldred's telling him ten times a day he should be the next prime minister that accounts for it. That is sweet music to my brother's ears, you must know. He realizes it will never happen, but I think it has always been a secret ambition. Well, it is only natural; every man wants to rise to the top."

"Some are not too exacting as to the devices they employ," he said, with a meaningful look that had nothing to do with Fordwich, nor was Lady Margaret so slow as to think it had.

"He is a self-seeking, unscrupulous man, Eskott. But family, cousins to us, that is how he got his foot in the door in the first place. Now he has got his entire body in with this business of acting as secretary to my brother."

"Maddie suspects nothing?"

"When you are in the state that poor girl is in, you see what you want to see. I could almost pity her, if I weren't so disgusted."

"What do you figure is his aim, to use

the family to get a good position, or to marry her fortune?"

"Both. If it were only a job he was after, I wouldn't mind. Of course she is attractive; I don't say he don't *like* her, but certainly he is making use of her, using her connections to climb the ladder. If he found someone he liked better, or someone richer, I expect he would drop her without so much as a second thought."

"There is a rumor he played a similar stunt on a young lady back home. I think I must investigate that matter more thoroughly. Maddie puts an innocent coloring on the incident, but perhaps if he actually jilted a girl . . ."

"She wouldn't believe a word of it if he did. You would have to put the girl under her nose to convince Maddie, and then she'd be more apt to believe Henry than the woman."

"Perhaps I have been working on the wrong angle. I have been trying to discover his character by means of his politics. Just what exactly is it he does for your brother? What sort of work?"

"Work connected with Fordwich's position on the Privy Council. He summarizes reports my brother hasn't time to read, writes letters for him, that sort of thing."

"Nothing of a more personal nature? Estate business?"

"No, no, the bailiff at the park attends to all that. He may scribble off an occasional note about something my brother wishes done, but it is mainly government work. In fact, he is paid by the government."

"I see. I have just determined the fellow is a liar at least. He indicated quite the opposite to me—estate work, with a little politics thrown in."

"I'll tell you who knows more about his private life than anyone is young Barker—the fellow they call Taffy Barker. He was visiting Aldred just before he came to London. He don't see much of Barker any longer, now that he is working."

"Taffy won't miss Sidmouth's ball. I'll make a point of having a chat with him."

"You're going to a good deal of trouble, Eskott. Is there any special reason . . . ?"

He looked at her with a rueful smile. "Does it show? After all these years, I thought I had learned to hide it. Even as an objective friend, however, I would like to help her. You don't abandon your friends when they are in danger. Such an ambitious man as Henry is dangerous."

"You don't have to convince *me*. *I* think he is a positive menace, but she won't listen to reason. All I have done is turn her against me with my nagging. She won't feel kindly disposed toward anyone who shows Henry up for the scoundrel he is either."

"True, I must tread softly. The heart always rules the head, especially when the heart is *in love,* whatever that cliché means. I have come to associate it with another four-letter word: *hell.* "

"I'll go to Sidmouth's do tonight with them, to try to keep her feet on the ground. I do nothing but harp at the poor girl lately, but then she is acting very badly. She is with him this instant, I know, reading over his shoulder."

"I wouldn't leave them too much alone."

"I am not worried about seduction. She ain't *that* far gone that she has lost her morals. He is at pains to keep up the *appearance* at least of a gentleman. As Fordwich has not turned him off, he would not be thinking in terms of bolting to the border for a runaway match."

"I wish he would suggest it. That would open up her eyes fast enough."

"Don't count on it. I'll go and ask her to drive out with me. If I catch cold, it will be her fault, and I shall insist she dance attendance on me."

"Good girl. I must be off now."

Lady Margaret shook her head sadly at his retreating form. What dependence could be placed on a foolish girl who took up with that rattle of an Aldred, when she had a fine fellow like Eskott dancing at her skirts these five years—more. No dependence at all. She turned and walked swiftly toward the study door.

Chapter 8

Lord Eskott sought out Taffy Barker at Lord Sidmouth's ball to see if he could discover anything amiss with Aldred's personal life. The necessary preliminaries regarding the state of their respective health and the fineness of the party were quickly covered.

"Your friend, young Aldred, is rising fast in the world," Eskott said at length, glancing to the floor, where Henry was performing an exquisite bow to Madeline during the course of the cotillion.

"Knew he had it in him," Taffy agreed. "Very capable, popular fellow at Christ Church. Best-liked man in his class. Don't believe he ever made an enemy."

"A man who has not made a single enemy at his age must have a very obliging set of principles, ones that change with the company he keeps," Eskott said, making a joke of it.

"Wouldn't say so," Barker answered, choosing to take offense at the jibe. "Haven't an enemy myself, so far as I know. Not what you'd call a real enemy. The Sanfords were put out with me that I didn't offer for Caroline, but as to enemies—no such a thing."

"Rumor has it Henry left a lady behind crying willow when he left," was Eskott's next venture.

"Agnes Dannaher? Devil a bit of it. She was the one gave him the rush. That is to say, her uncle did it for her. Aldred ain't well inlaid, but he'll do. Do very well for himself. How'd you hear about Agnes? But you're a friend of Lady Madeline, of course," he went on, answering his own question.

"Was he actually engaged to Miss Dannaher? You paid him a visit a while ago, if memory serves."

"No, never got so far as an engagement. Hinted him away before he came up to scratch, you know. He wanted to court her, but it was frowned upon. They'd have been more than happy to have each other, but the old uncle thought he could do better for the gel. Daresay he will too, despite her looks."

"Is she not well endowed? Physically, I mean."

"Between you and me and the bedpost, Eskott, ugly as a badger. Nice, lively, entertaining gel, but plug ugly." He screwed up his face and shook his head to indicate his repulsion at the girl's looks. "Not that Henry could find a fault in her appearance. You never want to hint it in front of him."

"Odd that he would have been dangling after an antidote."

"Love is blind, folks say. Well, half of the county is blind to Agnes's looks, and the other half is female, if you see my meaning. The fellows are all trying their luck, but Henry definitely had the inner track, till the uncle came down hard. Forbid the match."

"At Christmas?"

"No, earlier. He had spoken of letting

Agnes come up to town with Mrs. Aldred to visit Henry, but when Henry didn't land himself in the honeypot in London fast enough to suit them, nothing came of it. Henry had some hope when he left last month to visit home that the thing might be kept alive, but he don't mention Agnes now. I don't really know what happened. No denying Henry's taking his time settling into anything in the work line. Thought he'd be set up sooner than this. He's choosy though. Always was," Taffy said, then went on to more agreeable topics.

"Hear Prinney's in the boughs with his old flirt, Brummell, again. Something to do with snuff and the Bishop of Winchester. Heard the details?"

"Beau made a point of requesting the regent's servant to dump the remains of his box in the fire after the bishop helped himself to it without asking permission. The typical petty sort of bickering that occupies certain parties, who shall be nameless for fear of treason, when the affairs of state are in jeopardy."

Each gentleman was eager to get away from the other. Eskott had no more interest in gossip than Barker had in more serious subjects. They each spotted another friend at the same instant, and used it as an excuse to part.

Eskott was a little disappointed with what he had learned. In his own mind, Aldred was clearly a scoundrel, making up to an ugly heiress, and happy to be rid of her when he got his clutches on a pretty one; but alas, it was not considered dishonorable to try to advance oneself in the world by means of a good marriage, providing the heiress's family was agreeable. He had not behaved badly enough to stand accused of real treachery. He was too sly for that. Even while these thoughts ran around Eskott's mind, the cotillion finished. He advanced toward the edge of the floor to intercept Madeline and Aldred as they came off.

Before they reached him, they were accosted by another gentleman, who asked Madeline for the next dance. "I am tired to death," she answered merrily. "Henry and I are going to sit this next one out, and refresh our parched throats with champagne if we can find where Sidmouth is hiding it. I refuse to be fobbed off with that dreadful punch."

To see her behaving so badly, so unlike herself, and particularly to see her show her marked preference for her cousin, caused Eskott to scowl. Glancing up, Madeline noticed Eskott staring at her.

"Let us discover what has got dear Eskott in the hips tonight," she said to Henry, advancing toward him. "I expect Lady Susan is not paying you sufficient attention. Is that the trouble, Eskott?"

"It seems the style tonight for ladies to be rude in refusing to stand up with the gentlemen."

"Eskott always makes it a special point to disapprove of me," she explained to Henry in a playful way, while she clutched his coat sleeve.

"Not always. Only recently have I found cause to disapprove," he said bluntly.

"You need not interest yourself in what partners I choose to reject, sir. It is really none of your business. Let us get our champagne now, Henry."

Lady Margaret was fast advancing on them. "I see you are about to stand up with Maddie," she said, smiling her encouragement of this scheme.

"Indeed he is not!" Madeline countered quickly. "I am not dancing this set. Get the champagne, Henry."

"I'll go with you," Eskott offered, for his aim was to have a few private words with the young man. Henry did not object to this idea. In fact, he looked pleased with it.

"I don't see Wellesley here tonight," Henry said, glancing around the room. "I suppose you heard what the regent said of him? 'A Spanish grandee grafted on an Irish potato' he called him. It was presumptuous of Wellesley to aspire to the prime minister's seat after all."

"Is that why you refused his offer of a position?" Eskott asked.

"How the deuce did you know about that?" Henry asked, pleasantly surprised by the question.

"I told you, you are much discussed in our ranks, Aldred. Was it a good offer Wellesley made you?"

"It would have been good had he succeeded in his aim but as he did not, he is expected to resign his seat in the cabinet. Certainly Lord Fordwich thinks so. I don't see how he can go on serving under Perceval after his complaints."

"Lucky you didn't take his offer then."

"There was more than blind luck in it. I waited to learn the outcome."

"You don't want to wait too long to make your decision."

"Now don't start tempting me again, Lord Eskott. You know my partiality to *some* of the causes you espouse. Catholic Emancipation, for instance, I feel strongly about, as many of us do, including Fordwich. It is the Old Lady of Manchester Square who has squashed the excellent idea."

"Take care, Henry. Your talk is taking on a salty, Whiggish tone. It is more usually only we who refer to Lady Hertford as the Old Lady," Eskott said in an approving way.

"Well, if you have an *interesting* offer to make, Lord Eskott, I am not *irrevocably* rooted to either side yet. This scribbling I do for my cousin is only a stopgap measure to keep body and soul together. I had not the good fortune to be born the eldest son."

"What you need is a rich wife, my young man."

"That would be my last preference, to establish myself at the cost of my personal happiness. I am too young to be thinking in terms of a marriage of convenience."

"Not all heiresses are old and ugly."

"No, some of them are young and ugly," he said over his shoulder, accepting two glasses of champagne.

"Some few are young and beautiful," Eskott pointed out, hoping to hear from the man's lips some words regarding Madeline.

"Yes, those are the unattainable ones," he answered sadly, with a noble smile.

Eskott saw no hope of discovering more from this clever weasel. He took the wine back to Lady Margaret, and Henry and Madeline wandered off to be alone.

"Did you learn anything?" Lady Margaret asked.

"Less than will indict him; more than enough for suspicion," he decided.

"Exactly the problem. He *says* the right things, but what he *does*—that might be a different matter. If he approaches you *directly* for a job, that will be a good indication of his duplicity, for he spouts the Tory doctrine better than any of them now. If he turns his coat on Fordwich, there will be no possibility he will allow the match. It is only Aldred's parroting speeches that put him in such high aroma at home."

"A pity he wouldn't spout off there as he does in my company."

"Don't think to beguile him into it. He has more twists than a corkscrew. The pity of it is that if *you* offered him a good post, *you* would end up the villain of the piece.

He has us bound wing and leg. I was never so vexed with anyone in my life. We must think of something to expose him."

"We'll have to do it pretty damned fast too," Eskott added, looking across the room, to see Madeline and Henry just leaving. She was so wrapped up in him she failed to see two different sets of guests nodding and smiling at her. The ignored parties shook their heads as though to say, "She is in love. What can you expect?"

Being a man of conscience, Eskott took himself severely to task that night, after he left the ball. How much was jealousy coloring his opinion of Henry Aldred? The actual facts were that the fellow had been turned off by one heiress, and was now dangling after another. He was looking for a lucrative position, which was surely not immoral when a man was without independent means. He was being rather devious about it, playing one end against the other and misrepresenting the nature of his work for Fordwich. He knew of plenty who had done worse, and been called wily, or even plain clever. Not an admirable man certainly, but not really a villain at all. If it were anyone else but Maddie who mixed up with him, Eskott knew he would not give it a second thought. As it *was* Madeline, he could not seem to think of anything else. The direction of his thinking tended toward exposing Henry's weaknesses. With this aim in view, he continued visiting the Second Court of St. James, where he became less welcome to Madeline with every visit.

Chapter 9

"Good gracious, not another white gown!" Lady Margaret exclaimed when the parcel from the modiste was unwrapped.

"Henry likes me in white," Maddie countered, lifting the confection from silver paper to hold it before her in front of the mirror.

"That seems to be all that matters to you nowadays, what Henry likes. You make a laughingstock of yourself, returning to white gowns like a deb, when you have been in colors for close to a decade. It is only to make yourself look young for him. Well, it don't work, milady, I can tell you. You look a deal more attractive in deep shades, with your sallow skin."

"Yes, Auntie dear. I know Eskott has

been whispering in your ear his deep dislike of Henry, but I am not a deb, as you so frequently and kindly point out. As a well-seasoned old jade of twenty-five, I must be allowed to select my own colors."

"Twenty-six next month, isn't it?"

"Just so, and twenty-seven the year after, twenty-eight the year after that. Like the rest of mankind, I age a year every twelve months. Meanwhile, I am not quite over the hill."

"You are beginning to look it, in those pale things you wear," Aunt Margaret said, striding from the room in anger, and rattling the door after her one more time.

Madeline shook her head, mildly annoyed, no more. How was it possible to be angry with such a delightful world? She saw Henry every day, and nearly every evening. She worked with him over her father's correspondence, having a much better grasp of business matters after her long interest in Papa's work. They went to balls and routs and plays. She had made the acquaintance of Eskott's poet, the much-praised Byron, and found him charming. Had she not been so much in love with Henry, she might have managed to fall in love with him, as the rest of London was doing.

Henry was also involved in seeing the disreputable side of London. Like any new young buck on the town, he wished to see the gambling dens, the green room at the theaters where the actresses and dancers met their patrons, the Comus courts where the fellows went after a night on the town, to top off with a sing-song. This was a part of his education that he considered necessary and she tolerated. She had learned that Henry did not like being bear-led. Once a week he was let off the leash to go slumming with Taffy or some other gentleman friend. If the spot to be visited were not *too* disreputable, he allowed her to tag along. She had accompanied him to Mrs. Bristol's private gaming hall, for instance, a spot on the fringe of accepted society, where you could lose your money in a high style, with a dinner afterward. The crowd was roisterous, not her own set, but interesting and amusing for *one* visit.

On this particular evening in February, Henry's night to go slumming, he was taking her to the Pantheon for a masquerade party. The white gown Auntie Meg disparaged would be partially concealed under a blue domino, and her face covered by a mask of egret feathers. That she was going to the Pantheon at all was likewise to be concealed from her father and aunt, who would disapprove. Ostensibly, Henry was taking her to the opera, but concealed in her father's carriage would be a pair of blue dominoes and masks. She was as exhilarated as a schoolgirl sneaking a forbidden book into her dormitory as she passed the dominoes along to Henry for hiding. Her eyes were shining with pleasure.

"I begin to think you are not such a well-behaved lady as I had thought," Henry teased, slipping his arm around her waist to steal a kiss.

"Think again, sir. I expect you to protect me this evening. I hear the Pantheon has become disagreeably rowdy. I know I shall adore it."

"Hoyden! So shall I, when I am with *you.*"

"Oh, and the opera we are not seeing is *Martha,* if the subject should arise when we return. Eskott recommended it highly."

"Then it is bound to be a dead bore."

"Very likely. It deals with two English ladies who pose as servants and get themselves jobs at a hiring fair, only to discover their contracts are binding."

"Excellent preparation, Maddie. Better

let on we went to one of the routs we have cards for afterward, as I don't expect we'll be home before two."

"Milner's is likely to be a tight squeeze," she mentioned.

"We'll say we went there, and no one will be the wiser. What are your father and aunt doing this evening?"

"Papa stays home. He does not care for the opera, and is tired from all his work. Aunt Margaret never goes out if she doesn't have to. When I am so respectably occupied, she does not feel it necessary to accompany me."

"What a blessed relief it will be to be free of her for once. She guards you as though you were a deb on preferment."

"I know. She wearies me to death too, Henry, but I wish you would try to be a little patient with her."

"I *do* try, my dear. I would have given her a piece of my mind long ago if I were not trying so very hard to behave."

"About the expenses for tonight, Henry . . ." she began uncertainly. She knew Henry's stipend was small. As many of his expenses involved herself, she could occasionally induce him to take a little cash. But he disliked it.

"I have money," he said quickly.

"I know you have, but I turned in the opera tickets we are not using, and got a refund for them. Now *do* take it, please."

"Oh, very well, but I shall add it to my tally and repay you in full when I am higher in the stirrups. I hate taking money from a lady."

"I hope you don't take it from any other lady but me!" she teased, slipping him a larger sum than the imaginary refund of the tickets would have amounted to. He would so seldom take any that she was sure to give more than enough for the night's entertainment when he was in a taking mood.

"How can you even *suggest* such a thing?" he asked, offended.

"I didn't mean it, goose! I was only joking," she said, sorry to have hurt his feelings. Henry was so foolishly sensitive.

By the time her father's carriage deposited them at the south side of Oxford Street for the masquerade, their dominoes and masks were in place. The others entering were similarly attired, so that no identities could be distinguished.

"One would never take this for a haunt

of the rabble," she said, glancing at the magnificent structure.

"I daresay it is nearly as fine as Carlton House. Chandeliers, gilt, and glitter everywhere. When are you going to get me a bid to the regent's palace, Maddie? You have been promising it for an age."

"As soon as ever I can, but one cannot go there without an invitation, you know."

They hired a box and sat for a quarter of an hour, watching the show below while they sipped their wine. Their pastime was divided between holding hands and flirting with each other and making outrageous guesses as to what lofty personages were hiding behind the masks, and misbehaving below. "I bet that corpulent gent chasing the demi-rep in the low-cut gown is the Duke of Clarence," Henry said.

"Impossible. He spends all his time chasing ladies of fortune, for since he has turned Mrs. Jordan off, he means to set up as a respectable married man. *I* bet it is one of his brothers."

"You don't suppose the red-haired filly staggering toward the door is Caro Lamb?" was his next suggestion.

"I shouldn't think so. She doesn't drink to excess. It is a lightskirt. In fact, I think

147

all the women here are. Henry, I don't believe I shall dance after all. The place has got very rough and wild since I was last here a few years ago."

"My dear girl, you don't go to France and not drink the wine. Of course we shall dance. Am *I* not here to protect your fair name and honor? Come, drink up your wine. They are playing a waltz."

"But if anyone should recognize me and word got back to Papa . . ."

"Don't be an old prude, Maddie."

The word *old* could always prod her on to any foolishness, for it loomed much larger in her mind, that year's difference in their ages, than it should have. She was as sensitive about it as Henry was about the disparity in their social and financial positions. Not that he ever purposely brought the subject up; it was only at such minutes as this that it arose.

"Oh, very well, but if I am found out and ostracized from decent society, I shall hold you to blame."

They went below to join the dancers on the floor. With such a throng, even waltzing with Henry was no pleasure. Their elbows were constantly being hit; collisions occurred at every step. The heat too was unpleasant, while the level of noise was beginning to give her a headache. Henry, on the other hand, reveled in it all. For three-quarters of an hour it went on, till she could bear it no longer.

"Let us go back to our box and have another glass of wine," she begged, hoping from there to have him take her home.

When they got upstairs, their box had been taken over by a merrymaking group of bucks, accompanied by three females who looked like actresses, or worse.

"I'm afraid this box is taken," Henry said, in no impolite way, but firmly.

"So it is, my good man, by *us,*" one of the bucks replied. The crowd was tipsy enough to find this rejoinder highly amusing.

"I must ask you to leave. We were here first," Henry told him.

"First come, first served," one of the girls said, hopping up to vacate the box.

"Sit down, Belle," her escort ordered, grasping her wrist and pulling her roughly to her seat.

"Let us go, Henry," Madeline said at once, happy for an excuse to leave.

"We paid for this box, my dear, and we shall have it," Henry informed her. It may have been the wine, or perhaps anger, which caused his voice to deepen menacingly.

"Really, I do not want to stay at all. I have had a headache this past half hour."

"There, your ladybird has more sense than you," the first speaker said, talking over his shoulder to Henry in a dismissing way, as he reached for the bottle of wine.

Henry's hand went out, quick as a lizard's tongue, and snatched the bottle. "You can have this in another box, or you can have it over your head in this one, sir. Which is your choice?"

"Well, well, and just when I feared the party was about to get dull," the man said, arising with a slight wobble to face the challenger.

"Please come away, Henry," Madeline begged, clutching at his sleeve.

Henry pulled free of her fingers and struck the first blow, square on the man's nose. The women hopped to their feet, chirping in glee. Madeline had some fear the other two men would join in and thrash Henry soundly, but they considered themselves gentlemen, though she did not recognize them, and limited their support to shouts of encouragement.

A crowd had soon gathered at the door of the box, to heighten the commotion into a regular carnival. She did not know whether to be relieved or horrified when six waiters came struggling through the throng and pulled the brawling men apart. Henry's face was red from anger and blows, his hair disheveled, his jacket all askew. He looked like nothing so much as a belligerent, sulky young boy.

"I demand a constable," the opponent declared. "This man assaulted me."

He was roundly supported by five noisy patrons, while Madeline tried to hide herself in the throng, fearful lest she be discovered. Watchmen were never far from the Pantheon, where half a dozen brawls a night required their services. Before she could escape, one came forward to herd them all off into a more private room, the manager's office. She went along, mortified, but unwilling to strike out all alone through the unsavory crowd. It was the word of six against one, and in fact Henry *had* struck the first blow, though with some justification.

"Do you know who I am?" he demanded stiffly. "Lady Madeline, will you be kind enough to go home and inform Lord Fordwich what is going forward here?"

He did not read her appealing glances, meant to convey he should at all costs keep their true names out of the scandalous affair.

"Aye, tell the prime minister while you're about it, milady," one of the girls laughed.

" 'Twould be better to tell them at the watch house," the constable answered, unimpressed by fine boasts. Without more ado, Henry and his opponent were hastened off to the closest watch house, while the other five returned to occupy Henry's box and discuss the marvelous entertainment they had just viewed. Madeline stood alone in the manager's office with a clerk.

"Can I call you a hackney, mum?" the man offered.

"Call my carriage, if you please. Lord Fordwich's carriage," she added, wishing she had thought to use a different name when they had stabled it.

The clerk sprinted forward with the greatest alacrity when he heard the name. When he returned to accompany her to the door, she asked, "Where did they take the gentlemen? What will be done to them?"

"Now you must not worry your head, mum. It'll be a night in the watch house for your friend. He'll be admitted to bail, present himself with his solicitor or some character reference in the morning at Bow Street, pay his fine, and that's all there is to it. Never fear they'll imprison him. We get a half-dozen cases a week worse than this little scuffle. It's the wine that causes the mischief."

"What watch house?" she inquired, and got the address of the closest one.

"Will it be possible to get him out to-night?"

"If Lord Fordwich personally wished to intervene . . ." the clerk said, his incredulous voice telling her how unlikely he found this. She knew it was impossible to go to her father with the story. Quite apart from finishing Henry's chances, it would embarrass her father unbearably. No, she must find help in some other quarter. Upset, nervous, humiliated, and uncertain though she was, she squared her shoulders, thanked the clerk, and left.

Chapter 10

Her decision was not long being made. Eskott's was the first, the only name that popped into her head. She disliked very much to appeal to him, but knew she could not go herself, a lady alone, to a watch house. She knew too that Eskott could be imperious, arrogant, demanding, when the occasion called for it. He would get Henry out with no trouble. The greatest difficulty encountered was to discover where he might be passing the evening. It was not yet late enough that he would be at home, not even eleven o'clock. She discovered at his own home that he was at Milner's rout party, that same one she and Henry intended to say they went to. She did not have her card for it with her, but was admitted with no difficulty. Lady Madeline Morash was not likely to be refused entry, with or without a card. She waited in a small saloon while a servant fetched Eskott for her. She was unable to face the milling group.

He came within a minute, smiling with pleasure that she had sent for him, that he found her alone waiting for him. The smile faded as soon as she turned her troubled eyes to him. Her face was pale, traces of tears still drying on her cheeks.

"Eskott, help me," she said, arising, her hands stretched out to him.

"My dear, what has happened?" he asked, his voice sharp with worry. Her fingers, resting in his, were cold, trembling. "Come, sit down and have a glass of wine. It will calm your nerves. Was there an accident?" He tried to lead her to a chair, sustaining her with one arm about her waist.

She stopped, turned to him, shaking her head and screwing up her courage to tell him. "It's Henry," she said. His fingers tightened on her wrist, till they felt like steel.

"What has he done?" There was no longer any trace of concern in his voice, but only anger and suspicion. She could see the immediate change in him. Till then, she had not realized Eskott actually hated Henry. She knew he jeered at him, made fun of "the boy," but had thought it more a reflection on herself than anything else.

"He got arrested, at the Pantheon. He is in a watch house. We must get him out."

"He had the gall to send for *you* with such a message!"

"No, he didn't send for me. I was there with him. A fight broke out . . ." In disjointed statement, she told the degrading tale, feeling cheapened, debased to have been a part of it.

Throughout it all, Eskott didn't say a word. He listened, with that cold, hard, unsympathetic face. "Of course I cannot go to Papa. I wish Henry had not used his name," she finished.

"I should think not indeed! This is a fine mess he's landed you in. Well, the first move is to get out of here without causing a scene. I expect half the world has seen you in tears already, and is wondering what you are doing on the town in such a state. I'll have my carriage called. Stay here."

"Mine is waiting. I asked the groom to stand by."

"Come along then. What are we waiting for?"

He threw his greatcoat over his shoulders as they hastened toward the carriage. "St. James's Square. Spring 'em," he ordered John Groom.

"No, no. We must go directly to the watch house," she told him.

"You're going home. I'll handle Aldred," he said, pushing her rather roughly in and onto the banquette.

"Maybe that would be best," she decided, not reluctant to have done with this

156

night's work. "So you think you can keep Papa's name out of it, Eskott? And of course my own."

"That must depend on how much he has boasted of his connection with you. I hope this at last opens up your eyes to that creature. To have taken you to such a dive as the Pantheon! And for you to go with him, Madeline, passes human comprehension. I think you have lost the last of your wits."

"I had no idea it had got so rough. You must not tell anyone about this. It would ruin Henry's chances for a good position."

"What chances? He's turned down the three best offers he is likely to get."

"He has only turned them down to wait for something better. You need not look down your nose at him because he is a self-made man without your inherited advantages."

"He isn't made yet. He's nothing, and if he ever *does* amount to a row of pins, he won't be *self*-made, but manufactured by you. By God, I never thought I'd see the day lady Madeline Morash was lowering herself to such a depth. Rubbing shoulders with cits and rattles at Bristol's gambling den wasn't low enough for you. You had to go to the Pantheon and fall into a common brawl. I'm surprised you haven't taken to strolling through the lower corridor with the ladies of pleasure at Covent Garden, or reserving a chair in the green room, to be leered at by fops and dandies. In a *young* girl your behavior would be unfortunate but understandable. In a lady of your years and experience it is not only ludicrous but incomprehensible."

"There is no need to be satirical about it. If I'd known you were going to be so disagreeable, I would have asked someone else."

"Who, Maddie? What *decent* friends have you kept up contact with this winter? You never visit anybody, nor pay the least heed to anyone but Aldred when you go out. You've made yourself a laughing-stock. This is the last straw. I'll bale him out for your sake, and to save Fordwich the disgrace, but don't *ever* appeal to me again on Henry's behalf."

"It was an error of judgment going there. I admit it. He's young and inexperienced. *I* should have known better. If you want to be angry with someone, be angry with *me.*"

"I am. And I'll give you some advice I never thought I would hear myself give.

If you feel about him the way your actions lead me to believe, marry him. It will provide *some* excuse for the way you behave in public. Newlyweds are generally given a season's grace. The follies of a bride are more excusable than those of a spinster of your years. Aldred might behave with more discretion then too. He might have some concern for his *wife's* reputation. He obviously doesn't give a tinker's curse for yours."

"Oh, go ahead, vent your spleen on me. It will blow off steam, so you won't rip up at poor Henry."

This speech had the effect of shocking Eskott into silence. "Well, upon my word!" was all he could find to say. Before he opened the carriage door for her, he added, "I'll call on you tomorrow morning. I trust you won't trouble Fordwich and Lady Margaret with details of this spree."

"Of course not. Pray do not mention it to them. We let on we were going to see *Martha.*"

"I had already concluded there was some duplicity to the family in the evening's escapade. They would have had the good sense to lock you up if they'd had any notion where you were going."

The door was slammed, the horses bolted on down the road, and Madeline stood looking after it for a moment before entering the house. She was relieved that her father and aunt were not downstairs. She walked softly to her room to be alone and think.

She had little fear there would be any unpleasant outcome of the night. Eskott's discretion was to be counted on. Despite his ill-humor, she could depend on him for that. What she had to consider, to assess, was Henry. An unattractive side of his nature had been revealed at the Pantheon. His reluctance to oblige her in taking her home when she told him she had a headache, his dragging out of her and her father's names, indeed even his poor judgment in allowing himself to be embroiled in a brawl when he had a lady with him—all these were serious flaws. But what she had to determine was whether they were flaws of character or only due to his inexperience. She was slow to condemn him. He was young; he'd had no more idea than herself of what the Pantheon was like till he went. If he used her father's position to try to get out of a tight corner, it was hardly surprising. He had no way of knowing how vulgar it sounded, that it was simply not done.

It had been a poor display on his part, and she would tell him so. She would not allow him to decide, in future, what entertainments were suitable for them to attend together. If he did not like it, then she would just have to learn to live without Henry Aldred. It was a decision she could not have taken twenty-four hours previously. A little chink had formed in the armor of her love.

Chapter 11

Whatever Eskott said to Aldred, it proved marvelously effective. Henry came the next morning in an agreeable state of self-abasement, apologizing for his behavior and begging forgiveness. "I ought to be whipped for exposing you to such a disagreeable experience," he said, with more self-directed violence actually than humility. "What must you think of me? Will you *ever* be able to forgive me? I had no notion the place was so disreputable as Eskott says. Taffy told me he has often taken girls there—*ladies* I mean—for a lark. I thought it would be fun for us."

"It *was* disagreeable certainly, but the fault is not all your own. In future, I must follow my own judgment regarding where we can go together."

"I shall follow your judgment also on where it is acceptable for me to go alone. I come to see this idea we had of my taking an occasional night off was a perfectly wretched one. I have seen enough of the wrong side of London life that I want to see no more. It is only, you know, that I hear Taffy and the fellows talking about this and that spot—the green room at the theaters and so on—and I feel like the country cousin I am when I don't know what they're talking about. But there is nothing wrong in being a little naïve after all. That's all it was, Maddie. Just stupid country innocence."

"Did Eskott manage to hush it up?" she asked, weighing his words and finding much to agree with in them.

"Yes, he was wonderful. Came striding in, telling the world who he was, and that I was a most particular friend of his. He didn't seem to mind having *his* name used, Maddie, so I think you were a little hard to rip up at me for using yours."

"The cases are quite different. Eskott is a bachelor—he has no immediate family to be sullied if it should leak out. And if you think he did not mind, you are out in your thinking."

"At least it is hushed up. He came down pretty heavy to get my name off the books."

"We'll have to reimburse him. What is the sum?"

"He said not to bother with it. Five or ten guineas is nothing to him."

"It is a matter of honor, like a gambling debt. Naturally we shall pay him."

"I offered him last night, and he refused."

"You should have insisted. I'll find out from him what he paid, and reimburse him on your behalf."

"Be sure you let me know the sum, and I'll repay you. I don't mean to take any more money from *you*. That is something else I should not have allowed myself to do, or allowed you to talk me into doing. You must be more strict with me in future, Mama," he added with a smile.

"I mean to be, my boy," she answered, patting him on the head in a mock semblance of maternity.

The scrape was eased over with Eskott's help, and the lovers were back on good terms. Not quite so good as formerly, but they were still more than friends. Henry called her "Mama," till she hinted it had ceased to amuse, at which point he stopped at once, showing every sign of shock that she should take it amiss.

Eskott came the next morning to receive Madeline's thanks and to continue his scold. Henry was in her father's study when he arrived; she did not call him, instinctively feeling she could handle Eskott better alone.

"I owe you a large debt of gratitude, my dear friend," she said, walking to the doorway to meet him. On a sudden impulse, she stood on tiptoe and kissed his cheek.

"I don't care for the manner of repaying it," he told her. "When a young lady makes free of a gentleman's cheek in that way, it shows pretty clearly she considers him too old to appreciate a *real* kiss."

"It was a gesture. I mean to repay you in cash too. How much did you have to bribe the watch man?"

"The boy and I have settled that."

"No, you and the boy have not settled it to my satisfaction. You told him to forget it; he was too shy to press you, and has enlisted me to do it for him."

"He has already been here to explain, has he?"

"He works here, remember? He is in the study this minute."

"Then I shall settle the score with him before I leave. I had not realized he was encumbered with *shyness*," he said, taking up a seat before the grate.

"I'll get him," she said.

"Wait! Let us have a little private conversation first."

"You don't have to repeat last night's injunctions. Henry and I have had a good talk. He promises to reform; I promise to keep him on a shorter leash. *C'est tout.*"

"It is strange, you know, we used to find other things than Henry Aldred to discuss when I visited you. You will notice how I am curbing my tongue. I didn't say 'more interesting things,' but only 'other things.' Sit down; order some tea. It's demmed cold outside."

She pulled the bell cord before taking up a seat beside him. "So we did. As a matter of fact, I would prefer not to talk about Henry today. I am more than a little peeved with him. I see your young poet, Byron, is quite the rage."

Eskott entered willingly into a spiel in

praise of him. "The book I lent you is excellent, don't you think? I would like it back, by the by."

"I haven't read it! Everyone tells me it is all the crack, but I am more interested in his love life. Who is he chasing after this week?"

"He's never allowed to chase anyone. He is too busy running away from them. He blames his bad foot for the inordinate number of times he gets caught. Lady Ishington would like to appoint him her lover, they say."

"A highly unlikely appointment!"

"The poet mentioned Emperor Caligula appointing his horse a consul when the subject arose. I assume he cast himself in the role of emperor though. A cruel cut, considering the lady's unfortunately equine face."

"Papa mentioned seeing him at Carlton House."

"Yes, I thought I would see you at that do."

"One cannot go uninvited."

"Your father could have taken you, but I assume you mean Aldred was not asked."

"That was my meaning of course."

"You missed a famous do. Brummell was

widely quoted as inquiring of Weston who is acting the prince's taxidermist these days. He has got so broad one does wonder whether he is not stuffed rather than tailored. About your not attending, is it not possible to get a card for Aldred?"

"Till he has a decent appointment, one does not like to put him forward too much."

"Why the deuce don't you get him one then?"

Henry came into the saloon at that moment, bowing and uttering a dozen expressions of gratitude to Eskott, who brushed them all aside brusquely.

"I'll see what is keeping tea," Madeline said, excusing herself. Her true motive was to leave Henry privacy to repay Eskott.

This was not the subject that arose between them, however. When she returned, Eskott was saying, "It seems to me if the Tories can't find a place for you, you would do better to come to us."

"So that is what you're up to the minute my back is turned!" she accused Eskott. "Trying to steal my protégé."

"But of course! We could discover all sorts of interesting secrets from him, as he has been acting Fordwich's private secretary all this time."

"He is not privy to any state secrets," Madeline answered, knowing Eskott was joking. On this occasion, Henry made no mention of performing only estate duties for his cousin.

"Pity. We would give our ears to know what is going forth between Prinney and your set. We know Wellesley's bid was rejected, of course. As Perceval chose to word his letter to us, asking for our cooperation in forming a cabinet of all the no-talents, in the most insulting terms, we assume there is some other alternative being hatched, which excludes us entirely. Now if we could only figure out what the cabinet has in mind, we could be busy to stick a spoke in their wheel."

"You must be more subtle if you wish to weasel any secrets from us," Madeline told him. "Now that we know what you are up to, we shall be on our guard."

Henry listened, smiling, till the subject was dropped. "What are you doing this afternoon, Maddie?" Eskott asked when he was about to take his leave.

"Papa is speaking in the House. I plan to go and listen to him. I shan't say *see*

168

him, as the gallery you lords have chosen to set aside for females shows us nothing but the mace and the speaker's feet. All that crimson-draped throne and finery you keep for yourselves."

"But it is a nice private place for gossiping, and that is your real reason for going."

"We don't have to climb so many stairs into a dusty, dingy cubbyhole that is nothing else but a ventilator room to gossip, Eskott. We do that in comfort at home in our saloons. It is the wish to learn that takes us out."

"Is anyone going with you?" Eskott asked, with a little look in Henry's direction.

"Not I," Henry answered at once. "I shall be busy here."

"May I accompany you then?" Eskott asked.

"Certainly, if you like."

"Good. I can hear what is going on as well from the strangers' gallery as from my seat in the House, and don't really mind if I only see the speaker's boots. They have his phiz beat all hollow for looks. I'll call for you in a couple of hours, if that suits you."

When the tea was done, he took his leave. "This is not the first time he has spoken to me about joining his party," Henry mentioned.

"He was joking."

"I suppose he was. He never offered anything definite—specific, I mean—either time."

"It was a dig at me for doing so poorly by you. There is a do coming up at Ten Downing Street this week. I'll speak to my father about getting you an invitation. It is not like Carlton House in that respect. It can be arranged. You'll meet several people who have not been to call here, or met at other functions."

"I would appreciate it if you could. It is a waste of time, and demmed dull, writing to your father's constituents about roads and taxes. I thought politics would be more interesting."

"It will be, Henry. You haven't been initiated into the inner doings yet. If you were reading the dispatch boxes that come for Papa instead of his dull stuff from the county, you would be fascinated. I wish you could come with me this afternoon."

"Eskott will take care of you. He has earned some reward, after last night."

"Yes, but I would have a better time with *you.*"

This won her a hurried kiss before Henry returned to his work.

Chapter 12

Lady Madeline enjoyed her afternoon under the eaves of Westminster, despite the poor view of the proceedings below. Eskott put himself out to be entertaining. It was only her father's speech they listened to with any attention. The rest of the time she was beguiled with the latest gossip, a matter on which she had fallen behind in recent weeks.

"They say Mrs. Jordan is threatening to publish the Duke of Clarence's letters if he don't ante up a better settlement on her," Eskott mentioned. "That should make entertaining reading. Twenty years of them."

"What price is she asking for silence?"

"Fifteen hundred a year for herself, the same for the children, and all manner of perks. She won't have to display her aging charms on the boards, if she's successful. Sad all the same—twenty years shot to hell."

"She's thrown over, and *he* will take to himself a tender young wife."

"If he can find anyone to have him. The girls are turning him off in droves. Miss Long, Miss Mercer, Lady Berkeley, Meg Elphinstone. She is the latest he has in his eye. Lord Keith, her father, will never hear of it. As a seaman himself, he has too shrewd a notion of a sailor's morals."

"I expect he has a shrewd idea too that Clarence will never inherit the throne, or he'd hand her over fast enough, morals or no."

"It might be the young lady herself who objects. Your breed seem singularly uninterested in social advancement this season."

"Is that, by any chance, a reference to my cousin Henry?"

"Whatever gave you that idea?" he asked sardonically.

"I can't imagine, unless it is the sly way you said it. I wish you will quit casting out lures to him. He is such an innocent soul he half thinks you mean it."

"You are such an innocent babe, you think I *don't.*"

"Eskott, how horrid of you, trying to steal my beau."

"The fellow needs a decent position if

you mean to marry him. You are going to, aren't you?" he asked, regarding her with interest.

"We shall see. I may be more interested in my social position than you think. He will attend Perceval's do this Friday at Downing Street, to throw him in the way of any influential gentlemen he has not yet met. I expect something will come of it."

"If it don't, you can always toss your handkerchief at the Duke of Clarence. I wonder he hasn't been throwing himself into your saloon before now."

They drove through the park before returning home, though it was not a popular spot in the winter months. It was Eskott's aim to discover if she had definitely settled on Henry. He found her strangely evasive, which was at least better than a firm commitment. When he invited her out again the next afternoon, however, she declined.

"I'll see you at Downing Street on Friday then," he said, as he left her at her door.

Henry was wearing his new black jacket for that important occasion, and looked even more dashing and handsome than usual, but Madeline did not let herself be diverted by mere admiration. She instructed him on how to perform at the

173

prime minister's party. There would be gentlemen from both political sides there. He was to concentrate on the proper side, making a good impression on Perceval if possible. They went with Fordwich, and were admitted at the door by the porter. A steward draped in gold braid announced their arrival. They crossed the black and white marble floor to be received at the stairfront by Perceval and his hostess. Already the party was in progress.

"We shan't stick together tonight, Henry," she told him. "You stay with my father. Capitalize on this opportunity to make yourself known. Every person in this room is important. I might almost say every important person in town is in this room. I shall circulate and puff you off to anyone who comes in my way."

"There seems to be more Whigs than anything else," Henry said, scanning the crowd.

"Everyone is here. I expect the Tories take it for a business meeting, and are huddled in the library at the head of the stairs, talking politics. Papa will rout them out. Ah, here is Eskott," she exclaimed as he approached. "I'll have a dance with him, and meet with you later."

Before she broke away, Eskott joined himself to the party from St. James's Street. "What do you think is the reason for this sudden bout of hospitality on Perceval's part, Lord Fordwich?" he asked.

"No idea. The party came as a surprise to us."

"A farewell do, perhaps, as he will not much longer be in a position to offer the hospitality of Ten Downing Street?" Eskott suggested mischievously.

"Wishful thinking on your part," Madeline answered swiftly. "You had your chance for a *little* power, and were foolish enough to turn it down only because the P.M. uses a style of letter you do not like. The poor man can't help it if he expresses himself like a washerwoman."

"We are not likely to be contented with a *little* power, when the whole pie is within our grasp at last."

"I shall draw you away, before Papa has an attack of apoplexy," Madeline said with an apologetic look at her father. "Why must you say such things, inciting him to anger?" she chided as they walked toward the dance floor.

"He hears worse every day, if he is listening at all. Nice to see you behaving like your old self, and not sticking like a burr to your boy. His nose will be out of joint, not getting first dance with you."

"We did not come here tonight for pleasure."

"Was it for penance, as you voluntarily accepted my company? I shan't cavil. I am always happy to dance with you, whatever your reason."

She enjoyed the dance, and the easy company of an old friend who knew what subjects amused her. She was not amused, however, when Eskott soon pointed out that Henry had fallen into conversation with the enemy Whigs.

"The idiot!" she exclaimed. "I most particularly told him to talk to Eldon and van Sittart. Castlereagh too will probably come into an important post before long."

The word *idiot*, though spoken with feeling, was by no means an indication of lessening affection with Madeline. Eskott could not count the number of times she had castigated himself as one. Almost he was angry, to hear her speak so frankly of her new beau. "Who is the fellow he is talking to?" she asked. "I don't recognize him. Is he new, or just unimportant?"

"He's one of the bucks from Ireland.

176

Reed is his name. A head hunter for us, Maddie. You better go after Henry. Reed is more menacing to your cause than poor I, no matter how much you chide me."

She hastened forward to detach Henry from this menace, using the excuse of wishing to dance with him. She burned his ears for choosing so unhelpful a conversational partner, at this, his greatest opportunity. "I had no idea who he was! He accosted me. You must have seen it."

"I didn't notice. I was dancing."

"You never notice *me* once Eskott enters a room," he sulked.

"I thought you were with my father. I told you to stay with him."

"He's gone to play cards with a bunch of old fellows. That Reed chap agrees with Eskott that this will be Perceval's last do at Number Ten."

"Of course he does. He is a Whig. There—go and say how-do-you-do to William Lamb. You met him last week, remember?"

She did not dance with Henry after all, but circulated through the crowd, chatting to friends. She was busy throughout the evening to make Henry known to anyone who could help him, but of course nothing specific in the line of an offer would be mentioned at a polite party. Henry was rather disgruntled when they got back home, becoming impatient with the perpetual delays.

"You must do something for yourself, Henry," she pointed out. "I have got you an entrée to the prime minister's home. What do you expect of me, to dun him outright for a job for you?"

"Of course not. I appreciate your efforts. I didn't mean to cast any slight on *you.*"

"Well then, you have met everyone. Go to call on some of them tomorrow. Tell them you are open to an offer. Something will come from it."

"I am not in the custom of going, hat in hand, *begging.*"

"Maybe it is time you got in the habit then," she said angrily. Definitely Henry was less agreeable to her that night. He looked very sulky and was behaving with a childishness that displeased her. His conversation was not so amusing as Eskott's after all, or that of any of her old set.

"I'm sorry, love. It is only the delay that irritates me. I hoped we might be able to be married in June. I know we said a year, but seeing you every day . . ."

He put his arms around her, pulling her to him for a passionate embrace, murmuring soft words of desire and impatience. It was enjoyable enough to smooth her ruffled feathers, to make her forget his peevishness.

In the morning, there was a new development at St. James's Street. An unofficial cabinet meeting was taking place, to decide what was to be done about Wellesley. Perceval was not present.

"Wellesley has advised the regent to bring in Lords Castlereagh and Canning to strengthen the cabinet," Eldon told Fordwich, his head wagging in displeasure. "I for one am determined to resign if Wellesley does not. I hope we are all agreed upon it. If we act as one, the regent must accept our verdict. Our first allegiance is to our prime minister, and Perceval is still that. We owe it to the office, if not to the man. How is he expected to command, with Wellesley smirking at him from the corner, his resignation refused by the regent? The situation is intolerable."

"His resignation has been turned down once," Tilsit mentioned.

"A formality only, indicating the prince's wishes. Of course he can resign if he really wants to. A man can always claim ill health, use a gentleman's excuse."

"The prince might use it as an excuse to turn us out of office," Fordwich warned. "At this time, with the Whigs waiting like hawks to pounce, we would be better advised to use discretion."

His words, though listened to, were not followed. After an hour's heated debate, it was decided to present their ultimatum to the prince regent. They requested Perceval himself to come and do it. A part of the cabinet went with him, and the others remained behind to hear the outcome after Perceval returned. While they were still assembled, Eskott dropped around for a purely social visit with the ladies.

He noticed the collection of hats and gloves in the hallway, and asked Madeline, when he joined her and Lady Margaret in a smaller parlor, what was afoot.

"Nothing you would be interested in," she replied, with a laughing eye.

"Aha, the cat is in with the pigeons now. I cannot think what the old fellows are about, presenting their ultimatum in such stringent terms. Not necessary either. The prince would not be allowed to accept Canning, whatever about Castlereagh. Canning is adamant on the matter of Catholic Emancipation, and Hertford don't allow Prinney to approve of it this year."

"How did you know all about it? It only happened this morning," Lady Margaret exclaimed. "I didn't hear a word of it myself till I sneaked up and listened from the parlor next door. It is supposed to be a great secret, Eskott. Who is the spy, eh?"

"It was overheard last night at Ten Downing. The name Canning was being whispered in every corner and Castlereagh actually cropped out into a smile. He has teeth. I hadn't realized it before."

"The ministers are all too discreet to discuss it openly at a party. I daresay they have known it was coming for a fortnight, but the decision to resign if Wellesley don't was only made today."

"Well, now you see, I didn't know *that* was the deal. *My* understanding was that they would *threaten* to resign if Canning was invited in, and that was only conjecture, to be sure. We knew Perceval would insist on some hard action. His present position is untenable."

"You see how he learns our secrets," Madeline said to her aunt. "Now he will suddenly find he has to leave—he has forgotten to feed his cat—but his intention is to dart to Grey and Grenville and Brougham with the story. We must be more discreet in future, Auntie."

"To be sure we must, though it won't remain a secret for long if the resignation is accepted. Will it be, Eskott?"

"No such luck. Wellesley is too crafty to split the party wide open over himself. Too damaging for his future prospects. He'll leave, for the time being, and woe betide those who have opposed him when he does get into power. He'll resign, I expect."

"No woolsack for you this year, my friend," Madeline said.

"All things come to those who wait. Speaking of waiting, where is Henry today?"

"He is not working today. He usually takes Saturdays off to look after his own business matters."

"Having his curls trimmed, is he? As you are left alone and pining, might I induce you to come over and help me entertain a bishop this afternoon? A demmed dull dog, who is battening himself and his family on me for the week. You and Lady Margaret come to tea and amuse the ladies for me."

"I thought you would enjoy that part of the visit yourself," Madeline said with a pert smile.

"You wouldn't think so if you had got a look at the ladies in question. Bring your Bibles, and any stray hymnals you have lying about the house. Be sure to wear two or three shawls too, if you plan to appear in that dashing gown, Maddie."

"This modest old thing? Why there isn't a square inch of my sinful flesh showing. What's wrong with it?"

"It clings. It is clear to the most disinterested observer that you have a waist. The bishop's ladies wear theirs hanging loose. I suspect the daughter might have something worth seeing too, if she weren't so bundled up in blankets. I don't know whether it was her or her mama who draped my fine Grecian nude statue of Aphrodite in a shawl. I am blaming it on Maude, the daughter."

"Shall we oblige Eskott, Auntie?" Madeline asked. "We might as well. I have nothing better to do, and will end up ordering a new gown if I go to Bond Street."

Lady Margaret was delighted to see a new closeness springing up between Eskott and

Madeline. "We'll be happy to go. What time do you want us?"

"Three will be fine. Any gossip you can scrape together regarding the outcome of the visit to Carlton House will be very acceptable too. The ladies are interested in politics."

"No doubt you will tell us when we arrive what happened," Madeline said. "You appear to know as much about it as we do."

"We stop at nothing to find out what you are up to, in order to exploit all opportunities for making mischief. I may be sitting on that woolsack yet. I must go now and feed my cat. See you at three."

Madeline and Margaret exchanged a knowing nod at his true errand—off to report to Grey and Grenville. The little smile on Madeline's face caused her aunt to hope she was noticing how well Eskott looked that morning. The excitement of the pending cabinet resignation had lent a glow to his eyes, a heightening to his usually rather pale complexion.

"He would make an excellent minister, would he not?" Margaret asked innocently.

Her niece was not listening. Her next speech showed it clearly. "How did he know about the resignation? I'm sure it was not spoken of last night."

"He didn't *know;* he guessed."

"But how did he guess so accurately? I only had an inkling myself because I happened to look over Henry's shoulder at a letter he was writing for Papa that alluded to it. Even that did not use the word *resignation,* but *last resort,* which I took to mean resignation."

"There could be a leak in the ship of state. I have often heard your father tell of such a thing during the days of Pitt's— the younger Pitt's, regime. Thurwell was the fellow doing it, I believe. They caught him red-handed. Just as he was swearing to Pitt he was innocent, a page boy came in and handed him his hat—told him he had left it in some chamber where the Whigs were known to be meeting. Sheridan and Fox were in on it. What a storm it caused. Thurwell was after some great position for himself, and like the present situation, the government was expected to fall at any moment. It usually seems to bring the lower forms of bugs out of the woodwork, to scavenge for scraps. I'll mention it to Fordwich, and see what he thinks."

"Yes, I think we had better do that."

"It won't be necessary to mention *we* were goose enough to confirm Eskott's suspicions."

"I think not, but we must be more discreet from now on."

Chapter 13

They told Fordwich their fears. He was concerned at the possibility of a leak in the cabinet, but in the end concluded that none of his associates was capable of such wanton treachery as Eskott's knowledge would indicate. "Someone let an indiscreet word drop at Perceval's party. Parties are always dangerous, with so much wine flowing. We ought not to attend them when delicate negotiations are going forth. If he had been told by anyone, he would have had the thing straight. Our plan was not to resign if Canning was invited in, but if Wellesley did not resign. But he is resigning so that is an end to it."

Lord Wellesley was soon driving up to Carlton House in full dress, to hand the seals of his office over to the regent, who expressed every distaste for the business. This success went to the cabinet's head, and they began preparing other nasty surprises for the beleaguered prince. It was known in a vague, general way that something else was brewing, but the precise nature of it was unclear to the Whigs. The excitement was enough to give an old man, which Fordwich was, an acute case of indigestion. He was not so incapacitated as to be left out of affairs entirely. He was sent to his bed by the prince's own physician, Sir William Knighton, where his colleagues called daily and also dispatched to him vast boxes of correspondence to keep him abreast of developments.

The precarious state of the party did not restrict social doings in the least. Eskott still had two bishop's daughters and one wife to be entertained. They were vastly dull creatures, Lady Margaret declared, but she was agreeable to show them around the town when Madeline suggested it. Indeed she was pleasantly surprised at such condescension from Madeline. She did not realize Eskott was owed a special favor for having rescued Henry. She did know Henry was busier than usual with Fordwich home in bed, and sincerely hoped the absence of his handsome face would put him a little out of Maddie's mind. In fact, it took its other well-known course, and made her fonder of him, or at least lonesome for more of his company. She approved of his devotion to duty; it was heartening to see him pitch himself eagerly into the new load of work. There was a deal of running back and forth to be done, and Henry preferred trotting about in his carriage to sitting over a desk.

After the bishop's ladies had seen all the interesting churches, and a few dozen of the uninteresting ones, they were induced to join the more enjoyable business of touring the shops. It was after this last outing that Lady Madeline's carriage drew up in front of Eskott's house to deposit his guests at his doorstep.

"We'll just step in and say how-do-you-do to Eskott," Lady Margaret decreed, always busy to pitch Maddie into his company.

"He won't be home at five o'clock," Madeline pointed out.

"It is only a step. Let us go and see."

Eskott had just returned minutes before. "I stopped around at St. James's Street to see if you had gone back there," he said, welcoming them. "Have you shopped the stores empty?"

The few parcels being carried in indicated nothing of the sort; they were few and small. "Not quite," Madeline replied, with a little peep at the scanty packages. "But even window shopping is fatiguing. We would be happy for a cup of tea or a glass of wine."

"You have earned it," he answered, the swift, secret smile that passed between them expressing a whole outline of the afternoon's tedious rooting. "I didn't see Fordwich at the House today. I hope he is not ill."

"A slight indisposition," Lady Margaret assured him. "Nothing serious. It is business as usual, but from his bed. The red dispatch boxes are coming in thick and fast. Some new imbroglio going on."

"Don't bother perking up your sharp ears," Madeline warned. "We don't know a thing about it. Perhaps you can tell us?"

"I stopped by your place in the hope you would let fall some revealing remarks. We are all at a loss."

"Better go to Lord Minchin's ball tonight and see what you can hear over the punch bowl," Madeline suggested.

"Are you going?"

"No, with Papa feeling under the wea-

189

ther, we are using it as an excuse to stay home and get to bed before midnight for a change."

The bishop's wife opened her eyes wide at this telling speech. The conversation turned to topics that could include the ecclesiastical ladies till the tea was finished.

"I'll stop by tomorrow and see how your father goes on," Eskott said as he escorted the visitors to the door. His houseguests were already on their way up the stairs with their parcels. "Thank you very much for helping me. They say you are extremely obliging, which tells me you have had a very dull scald of it these past days."

"Not in the least. I have been meaning to count all the buttons in all the shops of London for some time now. Somehow I never got around to it. You know how it is," Madeline told him.

"You don't have to tell me; I owe you a favor."

"No, we are *even* now, dear Eskott," she answered cryptically. Her aunt frowned in curiosity, wondering what secret she was being left out of. The slyest questioning all the way home told her nothing.

The matter fell from her mind the moment they stepped in the front door of their own home. Fordwich stood in the hallway with his housecoat on, his hair all awry and his cheeks red with anger. The butler was the object of his tirade, which was in full swing.

"I tell you the letters have been opened!" he shouted. "The seals broken and very clumsily closed up again. I have left orders that the dispatch boxes are to be brought up to me the *instant* they arrive."

"Now Fordwich, calm yourself," his sister said. "Go back to bed. You'll catch your death of cold in this drafty hall without proper dress. What are you doing downstairs?"

"I came down the minute I got a look at this correspondence. How long was it sitting on that table by the door, for any chance caller to tamper with?" he demanded of the butler.

"I just went down to the kitchen to have a cup of tea, your lordship. I wasn't gone above half an hour. The downstairs footman said he would tend the door while I was gone. He was in the study dusting the top shelves, for the maids don't like climbing up the ladder. No one came except the courier from Westminster. The footman left the box for me to take up to you."

"Then it is someone in my own household who is spying," Fordwich decided.

"Rubbish, the letters were opened and resealed before they left Westminster," Lady Margaret countered. "Is there something very important in them?"

Fordwich did not actually reply, but his mutterings as he turned to the stairs to go back to his bed indicated that he had not actually taken time to read the letters.

"He is nervous as a kitten," Madeline remarked, looking after him.

"He's always on the fidgets when he is ill. All men are. I daresay the ministers have been worrying about their secrets since Eskott knew all about the great mass resignation. I'll go up and calm him."

When her aunt had gone, Madeline turned to the butler. "Is Mr. Aldred in father's study?" she asked.

"No, ma'am. He left an hour ago. Took some message to Lord Eldon for his lordship, I believe."

"Thank you. About the dispatch box, Evans—when did it arrive?"

"While I was at tea, ma'am. Less than an hour ago. Mr. Aldred was putting on his coat when I left. 'I'll see myself out, Evans,' he said to me."

"I see. Were you back at the door when Lord Eskott came to call?"

"Why, he didn't come, milady. I didn't let him in, and the footman said no one came. But then Lord Eskott doesn't always bother to knock, does he? He might have just stepped in, and seeing no one about, gone out again without disturbing us."

"That must be it. I spoke to him just now, and he told me he had been here. That's all, Evans. Tell Cook we'll dine a little late this evening. Papa will be having a tray in his room, and Lady Margaret and myself have just had tea."

After putting off her pelisse, she went to her father's room, to see Lady Margaret and Fordwich in quiet, worried conversation. "What's the matter? Was there something important in the box?"

"Yes, information we would not wish the opposition to get hold of just yet. I've told Meggie, and I don't mind telling you, Maddie, as you are not going out anywhere this evening, and soon it will be public knowledge. Do not speak of it to anyone. The fact is, Perceval is at loggerheads with the prince over Lord Sidmouth's appointment as lord president of the Council."

"Is that wise, Papa, to push Sidmouth

forward? The prince hates him—his father's prime minister. Sidmouth is generally blamed for not giving the regent his military promotion, which he wanted so much. Why must it be done at this time?"

"Perceval's doings. Sidmouth is able and conscientious—a good man. We can use him. The fact is, the prince is quoted here as saying he has no confidence in Sidmouth and, more significantly, that he has no confidence in any person who forces Sidmouth on him. If the Whigs have got hold of this piece of information—if they should decide to hold their hand on the matter of Catholic Emancipation, for instance, they could surely get themselves appointed as the government tomorrow."

"Why does Perceval persist then?"

"He means to show he has the upper hand, that he is not a puppet to anyone. Perhaps he has Lady Hertford's support, behind her hand as it were, but in any case, you can see we do not wish our enemies to know what we are about till the thing is done. Send for Aldred. I'll dispatch a note to Westminster and let them know about this affair—the letters being tampered with. They'll be there till all hours tonight if I know anything."

"Yes, do that, Fordwich," his sister said. "You'll hear they had some reason to open the letters themselves before sending them to you, and did not bother to put on a new seal."

"I think not. There are no cross-outs in the letters. I am going to get dressed. Call my valet, Maddie."

"A tempest in a teapot," Lady Margaret said to Madeline as they returned below-stairs. "Where is Henry? Will he be dining with us?"

"Probably not. Papa wants him upstairs now in any case. Evans, has Mr. Aldred come in yet?"

"Yes, ma'am. He's in the study."

"Send him up to my father, please. Papa will want him to go off to Westminster."

It was a full hour before Aldred returned. When he came back from Westminster, he had Lord Tilsit and Lord Eldon with him. Fordwich was dressed and awaiting them in his private study. The ladies and Aldred were excluded from the discussion that went forth. There was no shouting, no vocal sign of anger, but the closed door told them the matter was troublesome. After perhaps fifteen minutes, Mr. Aldred was sent for.

"They cannot think *Henry* had anything to do with it!" Madeline said to her aunt, outraged at the notion.

"He was here. He handles your father's correspondence."

"He doesn't handle the dispatch boxes, except perhaps to pass them on to Papa. And he wasn't here when it arrived either. Evans told me he had gone out."

"Maybe he came back."

"Yes, and maybe Eskott took a look while he came slipping in, unannounced. He was here; he told us so, remember? But Evans and the footman say he did not knock at the door."

"He often comes in without knocking."

"Yes, to see what he can learn at keyholes."

"Don't be absurd!"

Before their conversation had quite deteriorated into a fight, Aldred was back. "What a brouhaha! They've got the footman up on the mat now, trying to discover if he knows anything. The letters had not been opened and resealed before their departure from Westminster. Unless the courier has turned spy, it looks as though it happened here. A clumsy enough job too. The work of a servant, if you ask me. I daresay half our servants are serving the Whigs, if the truth were known."

"I cannot think so, Mr. Aldred," Lady Margaret said stiffly, bristling over his casual *"our* servants." "Our servants have been with the family for years, and in most cases, their parents before them. Servants do not concern themselves with politics in any case. It is nothing to them." With a truly blighting stare, she arose and swept from the room, to stroll slowly past the closed study door, trying to overhear what was passing within.

Henry turned to Madeline. "I hope your father does not think *I* had anything to do with it," he said.

"Of course not. You weren't even here at the time. He had already sent you on an errand, had he not?"

"To tell the truth, I didn't notice if the red box was on the table when I left. It might have been."

"It wasn't. Evans says you were already putting on your coat when he went downstairs for tea, and the box had not arrived yet."

"Yes, but I didn't leave immediately. I went back to the study to get some letters of my own to post while I was out. I stopped and had a few words with the footman who was dusting—just teasing him a little about that maid he is always ogling, you know. Then he left the room for a minute, and I collected and sealed up my letters. There was no one in the hallway when I actually left. Eskott's carriage was just drawing away when I got on to the street. I recognized it, but I'm afraid I didn't notice whether the dispatch box had come while I was busy in the study. You don't suppose Eskott . . . ? No, of course he would not. He is too fine a gentleman to do such a thing. What *is* the great commotion all about anyway? What was in the box, that they are so upset about it?"

Madeline was about to tell him when she changed her mind. "I don't know. Some highly secret business, I assume. Something the Whigs would turn to their advantage if they knew of it. You're *sure* you can't remember whether the dispatch box was there when you left? Red—it stands out. You would have taken it up to Papa before leaving if it had been there."

"I can't be positive. I was distracted at your seeing so much of Eskott, to tell the truth. I haven't said anything, Maddie, but—well, you *are* seeing a good deal of him lately. That was on my mind. Some little corner of my mind seems to remember, but I can't be sure the box was there. If it was *not,* then of course it cannot have been Eskott who tampered with it."

"No, it cannot." And it cannot have been *you* either, she thought to herself.

"Unless he spotted the courier as he drove away, and came back, knowing the hallway was unattended," he added reluctantly.

"It would be attended when the courier knocked on the door, Henry. *He* would not enter unbidden," she pointed out.

"That's true. He would have had to wait till the footman left, and there would be no saying the box was not taken immediately to Fordwich, as it should have been. I personally cannot think for a minute Eskott would do such a thing. I place my money on the servants, your aunt's prejudices notwithstanding."

Lady Margaret returned to them, no wiser than when she had left. Nothing could be overheard through the door except Fordwich sneezing his head off. He was coming down with a cold; that was why he felt so wretched. They'd all get it. Before she sat down, dinner was announced.

"Will Lord Fordwich be joining you, as he has left his bed?" the servant asked.

"I doubt he'll be finished before midnight. We shall eat without him," Lady Margaret answered.

"I am leaving now," Henry said. "Your father does not need me. As you told me you were staying home, I made plans to dine with Taffy and some friends at one of his clubs. I shall be back tomorrow bright and early, to discover what happened."

"Thank God for that," Lady Margaret said when he was gone. "This evening will be vile enough without his chattering."

Madeline glared mutinously, but said nothing.

Chapter 14

There was little conversation over dinner. Madeline was trying to decide whether Eskott could possibly have wanted badly enough to know what was transpiring at Downing Street to open letters that did not belong to him. There was no denying he was ambitious. He wanted that woolsack very much. The Whigs had been waiting endless years to form the government. This was the best chance that was likely to come their way. If the prince regent did not bring in his erstwhile friends now, when would it ever happen? They all knew it, and were furiously frustrated. And if that red box had been at the door when he came . . . The only other possible culprit was Henry, and why would *he* bother to risk so much to open letters he would soon have easy and proper access to? He was a Tory; there was nothing for him to gain by this underhanded trick. She wondered if Eskott had put Henry up to it, for she knew that vague hints had often been proffered to her cousin by Eskott. But if that were the case, Henry would not have mentioned Eskott's being at the house. Had she mentioned it first? No, it was Henry who'd volunteered the information.

Aunt Margaret chatted on about the malign influence of a cold on one of Fordwich's years, about returning to Highgate Park, and about the bishop's wife and daughters, while Madeline answered in monosyllables. It had to be Eskott. Nothing else made any sense. She had not a gentleman's strict ideas of honorable behavior, but she knew this was conduct heinous enough to ruin his reputation, at least amongst the Tories. If the Whigs were able to come into power by acting on what he had learned, on the other hand, she doubted very much he would long wear the guise of a villain.

When dinner was over and the ladies retired to the Gold Saloon, Fordwich and his cohorts were already there, having a glass of wine.

"The ladies know all about it," he explained. "I trust my own family's discretion. They do not go out this evening."

"Do you trust your cousin's boy equally implicitly?" Lord Tilsit asked blandly.

"What would be the point of his snooping? He is one of us. Certainly I trust him. What we must decide is whether to pull back on the matter of Sidmouth's appointment as lord president of the Council. It is a risky business. The appointment could always be made later."

"Sidmouth would never sit still for it. He still has his own circle of influence. Prinney already knows we want him. The fat is in the fire," Eldon said fatalistically. "If the Whigs come up with an acceptable cabinet—if they back down on some of their less attractive policies—I fear we are for oblivion."

"We must count on the influence of our friends on Manchester Square," Tilsit said.

"Thank God Lady Hertford still has something to say about it," Eldon added.

Into the midst of this controversy, Lord Eskott's presence was announced by the butler. He entered, outfitted in black formal clothes for his night's activities. A mischievous smile sparkled in his eyes as he looked around the room, where every face wore a frown. "A small caucus to discuss the imminent demise of the government?" he asked leadingly. "I think it excessively poor decision-making on Perceval's part to put Sidmouth forward so soon after dispensing with Prinney's bosom beau, Wellesley. But then you Honorable Gentlemen excel at the fine art of making bad decisions. Good evening, Lady Margaret, Maddie. Got a chair for a Whig, or shall I be discreet and retire?"

He was soon aware that the latter was the wiser choice. The men glared at him with open hostility, while Madeline's eyes narrowed in conjecture. How did he *know*, if he had not read the letter?

"May we know how you come to be so well informed of private matters, Eskott?" she asked.

"Private? It is quite publicly discussed at Brook's I assure you. Did you hope to keep such a choice tidbit secret? Not much chance. The prince regent is blubbering all over his mistress's bosom what a foul trick you hope to play him."

"I cannot think Lady Hertford told anyone she does not trust," Tilsit suggested.

"Then it seems she must have misplaced her trust, does it not?"

"It seems to *us* the affair was not circulated by Lady Hertford, but by someone else," Madeline said.

"Some demmed Whig like myself, you mean?" he asked, enjoying their discomfort.

"Precisely!" she shot back angrily.

Eskott looked at her, realizing there were some undercurrents here he had not fathomed. "Perhaps you would be kind enough to tell me your theory in this regard?"

"It is not theory but a *fact* that my father's dispatch box was pilfered this afternoon. His letters were opened and perused, then clumsily resealed."

"I am dismayed to learn state secrets are left lying about the house unguarded. When and how did this occur?"

"It happened here sometime around the

hour of your visit, Lord Eskott," she answered.

"That is a highly provocative statement, ma'am," he answered, his voice becoming tense with indignation. "There is at least an inference in there that *I* was the one to do the tampering."

"I don't know who else it might have been!"

"Do you not? I must say someone else occurs to *me.*"

"We do not have other *Whig* callers, Eskott, and obviously this is not the work of one of our own," she answered hastily, knowing he referred to Henry.

"In fact you are accusing me of opening private and confidential correspondence directed to someone else?" he asked, his voice nearly inaudible with incredulous ire.

She tilted her chin an inch higher and glared, saying nothing. Eskott was suddenly on his feet, his glance slowly circling the room, finally settling on the three distraught lords, every one of whom wished to give Madeline a sound shaking. Her aunt said angrily, "Shut up, you foolish girl!"

"Am I to understand you gentlemen share the young lady's suspicions?" Eskott inquired, his tone haughty.

There was a general, hasty, unanimous disclamation of any such view. "Nothing of the sort!" Tilsit exclaimed.

"Certainly not *my* interpretation of events," Eldon averred, scowling at Madeline.

More to the point, Fordwich said to his daughter, "You will apologize at once for that impertinence, Madeline."

She regarded him, stunned into momentary silence by the angry reaction she had evoked. Her father did not often speak to her so harshly. When he did, she obeyed unhesitatingly. "I'm sorry," she said, but with neither feeling nor conviction. It was the automatic response to her father's command, and she looked at him even while she spoke the apology. Then her glance went to Eskott. She had never seen such a face on him before. He was white-lipped with fury, the nostrils flared, the eyes two burning coals that bore through her, accusing, outraged, almost unbelieving. She waited for what seemed an eternity, half fearing he would walk forward and strike her.

Finally he spoke, suppressing all the violence that wanted to pour out. "I accept your apology, ma'am. Pray excuse me now, gentlemen. Lady Margaret." With a slight ducking of the head toward her aunt, he strode swiftly from the room.

"I don't see what he is so angry about," Madeline said.

"You will go to your room at once," her father commanded.

Still frowning, she arose and left. Eskott was just having his coat put over his shoulders by the butler. She hastened her steps toward him. "Eskott, I . . ."

He stared at her. "Good evening, Lady Madeline," he said. Then he accepted his hat with a show of indifference, pushed it down on his head, and left, without another glance at her, though she stood waiting for him to say something more.

She went up to her room to reconsider the meeting. She was there five minutes later when her aunt came storming in. "I hope you're happy now! All we need is for your poor father to have to fight a duel, and him already sick with worry about the state of affairs."

"Fight a duel? What are you talking about?" Madeline asked, blinking. "You mean with Eskott?"

"You don't call a gentleman a deceiving scoundrel without paying for it, Madeline.

If you had not apologized . . . Well at least you had that much common sense. This is all Henry Aldred's doings. I feel it in my bones."

"There would be no point in his having done it. Papa does not suspect him either."

"Maybe not, but he knows full well it was not Eskott, and so do you."

After a lengthy deliberation, Madeline convinced herself no one had opened her father's letters at all. She was sorry she had accused Eskott of it without thinking what she said, but only rising to his taunt that Henry was the culprit. He would be in a snit for weeks probably. No matter, she would bring him around her thumb, as she always did. She did not wish to lose his friendship. She would be especially nice to him the next time he called.

Before she retired, her father came up to read her a great, thundering scold for her impudence in speaking so rudely to a caller in his home. "As though Eskott would do such a thing. We have known him any time these thirty years, and his family before him for eons. I was never so embarrassed in my life, to hear you make such a wicked display of yourself. We may count ourselves fortunate this did not end in the court of twelve paces. It is only my advanced age and Eskott's common decency that prevented it, and not that tight-lipped, insincere apology you were pleased to offer. We'll not see *his* face at St. James's Street again. I'll be ashamed to meet the man on the street. You will write him an apology, Madeline, and enclose it in a letter with mine."

"I have already apologized. There is no need for you to do it, Papa."

"You are my daughter. I must take the responsibility for your actions. I am grievously disappointed in you. Write the letter, and show it to me before you send it off. I don't know what excuse you may find to offer. I personally can think of nothing to account for your inexplicable behavior."

"You overlook the fact that someone opened your letters, Papa. If not Eskott, then who?"

"That remains to be discovered. It cannot be left hanging like this. I should think Eskott's speaking so openly of his knowledge in front of us must have told you he was innocent, if your trust in his character did not. It is a fine kettle of fish. And just when I had hoped . . ."

"What?" she asked, curious.

"Why to tell the truth, Meggie had led me to hope he might be in the way of offering for you again. He stops by often enough. It is high time you were settled into a home of your own. I won't live forever, and you need not expect my heir to open his doors to you. You never rubbed along with your Morash cousins."

"But Eskott is a Whig!"

"What of it? He is a gentleman, extremely eligible. I do not despise any man for sticking to his principles, even if they differ from my own. There is something to be said for Brougham's boys after all. They want to rush pell-mell into the future, instead of inching slowly forward, but that is because they are young—younger by and large than our party. They are the future. Changes must come. Even the most reactionary of us realize that. If I were younger . . . But I am not. I am too old to turn my jacket on my old friends now. And so are you getting on in years, milady. You are too old to be playing the flirt. Rid yourself of Aldred's company, and settle on someone respectable while you still have enough youth to nab yourself a good husband. Not Eskott, alas."

He sighed wearily, looking every one of

his more than seventy years. Her heart went out to him. "I'm sorry, Papa," she said humbly.

"I should hope so," he answered gruffly, and left.

Chapter 15

A probable reason for Henry's having spied on Lord Fordwich soon came to light. A positive confirmation that he was indeed the culprit followed hard on its heels. He did not appear at St. James's Street on the following morning, but sent a stiff note informing his lordship that he had accepted the candidacy for a riding close to his own home, arranged for him by a friend of his father's. It was as a Whig he was running, or being appointed, for it was another of those rotten boroughs he mentioned. He expressed every civil gratitude for the kind attentions shown him by his cousins, et cetera.

"The turncoat!" Lady Margaret declared when her brother showed her the missive. "It is clear now why he was dragging his feet in accepting any position you found for him. It was his intention all the time to revert to his father's party. *Using* us, and causing a deal of mischief into the bargain. It must be Aldred who read your letters, and sent the word to his Whig conspirators, don't you think, Fordwich? That is how Eskott heard of it, but he did not realize the source."

"It begins to look that way. There are plenty of underhanded types in both parties who would not flinch at such a stunt. He was at Westminster for me yesterday. I'll make inquiries and try to discover if he was seen talking to any of them."

"You'll not go out with that cold. You're sneezing ten times an hour."

"I must. Send word to the stables to put in some heated bricks, and warm me a blanket there by the grate, Meggie, if you please. Where is Maddie?"

"Upstairs. Give me Aldred's letter. I'll be happy to show it to her. This will cure her."

"Cure her? You are not still prattling on that idea she has a *tendre* for Aldred!"

"You would have had him for a son-in-law before the year was out, if it were not for this letter."

She laid his blanket out by the grate, gave word regarding the hot bricks, and pranced upstairs, happy to be the bearer of such ill news for her niece, when its eventual outcome must be beneficial to the girl's welfare.

"I don't believe it!" was Madeline's first reaction. "He wouldn't do this to me. He couldn't . . ."

"No, and couldn't go snooping through your father's private correspondence either, I suppose? Well he has done it, and good riddance say I."

A letter was soon being slipped out the back door by the good graces of a footman. It was directed to the Albany, and requested in rather peremptory tones that Aldred present himself at St. James's Street at his soonest convenience to meet Lady Madeline. It was not the man but a letter that came an hour later, explaining that Mr. Aldred was no longer in the employ of Lord Fordwich, and any further meetings at St. James's Street were unlikely. Any further correspondence must be delayed, as he was leaving that same day for home, to meet with his new sponsor, Mr. Leadbeater. The name was not recognized by Madeline. She had never heard it, did not know he was the uncle of Agnes Dannaher. In fact, she did not know even the girl by name.

There was not a word of love, or explanation, or apology. "Naturally our former plans, vague and tenuous as they always were, will be ineligible now, as lord Fordwich will dislike my suit, but my principles must take precedence. I know you will agree with me in this. Sincerely . . ."

The more she read, the more indignant she became, till at last she could hardly hold the sheet steady. Principles indeed! His only principle was self-advancement. Something or someone had convinced him he would get ahead sooner on the left side of the House. That was his great principle. No doubt there was an heiress in the picture somewhere. A rapid survey of her friends and acquaintances led her to Taffy Barker to ascertain this point, but she was too ashamed to send for him. She would ask him the next time they met socially. The likeliest place to meet him that week was at Lady Wethercotte's rout party.

She was on the fidgets all day, unable to settle down, or even sit down. She paced about her room for an hour, then went belowstairs to pace the length of the Gold Saloon, reviewing the history of her association with Henry, and finding a fresh insult at every turn. She had taken a greenhorn from the country, got him properly outfitted and housed, introduced him to everyone, personally sponsored him into the ton, got him two or three good offers of employment, and this was her thanks. He turned and bolted on her the instant he got an offer he liked more. The offer was no better than the first one from Tilsit he had turned down either. Only an M.P. for a small borough. What was there in it that he should snap it up so fast? She had the liveliest suspicion that there was a girl, and a rich one, mixed up in the plot somewhere.

In the end, she decided to drive down to Bond Street just to get out of the house. Lady Margaret, who had promised Fordwich to keep an eye on the girl, went with her. They had done no more than alight from the carriage and walk a block before Taffy was spotted across the street, lounging on his malacca cane as he peered in a window display at a collection of snuff boxes. He was with another gentleman whom Madeline did not recognize. The speed with which Madeline flew across the street, without even looking to see if a carriage approached, set her aunt off on a series of clucking admonitions.

"Mr. Barker, I forbid you to buy another snuff box!" Madeline said playfully. "I know you have a round hundred of them. Are you setting up in competition with Lord Petersham?"

"Oh hallo, Lady Madeline, ma'am," Barker said, turning to speak to the ladies. He made his companion known to them, a Mr. Barker also, a cousin from the country. After a few complaints about the cold weather, the more interesting topic of Mr. Aldred was brought up by Barker. "Daresay you was pretty surprised to hear of Henry's marriage," were the first words spoken on this subject.

"Marriage!" she exclaimed, in accents that revealed all her astonishment.

"Why you cannot mean he didn't tell you! Dropped around to see me last evening. All set. He goes off to Manchester today. Merry as a grig. Well, he has been fond of Agnes forever, of course. Her old uncle Leadbeater gave him little hope, but the girl went into a steep decline, forcing her uncle to condone the match. Old Leadbeater is happy to have rescued him from the Tories into the bargain. It will be one more vote for the brewers. Agnes owns a brewery you must know. Rich as

Devon cream. A good match for your cousin. You must not fret he is throwing himself away. Henry spoke of getting a special license. I was invited up to the do, but don't like to make the trip in the dead of winter. I'll pay my respects to the bride when they get back to London."

"When is that likely to be?" she asked, assuming a pose of polite curiosity.

"Not immediately. They're having the treacle moon in Scotland, to visit the girl's maternal relatives. Deuced bad time for travel. Don't know why they didn't wait till spring, but I expect Agnes would not be put off any longer. Afraid she'd lose him."

"To the Old Lady of St. James's Square," the cousin said with a laugh. "Some elderly female took a sharp interest in Aldred, was forcing her attentions on him. I think it was as much to escape her clutches as anything that Henry rushed the thing forward," the cousin said, all unaware that he was saying anything amiss.

It came with the force of a sharp blow to the heart. Madeline felt physically ill with mortification. Henry had been laughing about her to his friends, making fun of her behind her back, intimating that she was forcing her attentions on him. The awful chagrin on Taffy's face, the open-mouthed horror, told the story too well. He stared helplessly from his cousin to Madeline to Lady Margaret, trying to think of something innocent to say, to cover the devasting truth just uttered.

"Heh heh, a little joke you know," Taffy said, rifling his mind for any single aging female on St. James's Street that he might pretend the reference was to. "Didn't mean *you*, Lady Madeline," was his best effort at mitigating the insult.

"It must be me he referred to," Lady Margaret said with an ironic smile, while the cousin looked totally puzzled, unable to imagine what the dashing young female he spoke to could have to do with Aldred's "managing old female."

To cover the gaffe, Taffy rushed into other matters. "You will not be best pleased at his reverting to his old Whig stand, but the Aldreds have been of that stripe forever, you must know. His papa cut up something dreadful."

"To tell the truth, Mr. Aldred never pleased us overly much," Lady Margaret said, in her grande dame manner. "Shall we be running along, Madeline? The wind is so chilly here on the street. Good day Mr. Barker, and Mr. Barker," she said, nodding to the two cousins in turn, before getting a firm grip on her niece's elbow to pilot her into the shop that purveyed snuff boxes.

"You dough-head!" Taffy was heard to castigate his companion.

"But surely *she* can't be the Old Lady . . ." The damning voice petered out to silence as the door closed.

"I'll *kill* him!" Madeline said between clenched teeth as she looked out at their rapidly departing forms, but of course it was Henry she meant.

"It would be a benefit to the world if someone would. Stay here. I'll see if the store has a boy we can send for our carriage. You'll want to go home to lick your wounds in private."

Madeline sat like a stone statue, silent, staring, during the drive home. Though she looked as if she might have frozen in the chilly winds, she was in fact a very active volcano inside. She was not high-minded enough that vengeance formed no part of her plans. She would dearly have loved to avenge herself on Henry Aldred, but her most wiley schemes were incapable of fulfillment. He was not here; would not be here for some time. He had jilted her; told the world he was doing it, then darted off and left her to face the taunting laughter. She wanted to crawl into a hole and hide for a decade.

"So what do you mean to do about it?" her aunt asked, when they had reached the comfort of their own saloon.

"What *can* I do? The coward has removed himself from my wrath. Till he comes to town with his bride, I can do nothing. And it is not her I wish to embarrass in any way. She'll have hell enough in her life, married to that scoundrel. There's nothing I can do but smile and pretend to like it."

"That's the spirit!" Lady Margaret said, relieved at this good sense. Indeed she was hard pressed to conceal her glee at the whole development. Any course that saw Madeline free of the young man was pleasing to her, and if a little embarrassment was thrown in—well, it wouldn't do her any harm to have her crest lowered an inch. "Just go about your business as before, and pretend you don't care two straws."

"I'll ask Eskott to take me to Lady Wethercotte's rout party this evening."

"That you won't, my girl," her aunt said

swiftly and firmly. "You may count yourself lucky if he *speaks* to you in future, let alone takes you to routs and balls."

"I apologized twice—once orally, and once in writing. Eskott is not one to hold a grudge, Auntie. We quarrel more often than not, but he always comes back."

"Not this time. Don't ask him, Madeline. Don't lay yourself open to further humiliation. Listen to me this time. I was right about Aldred, and I am right about Eskott. We old ladies *do* know something."

"Eskott always forgives me. He scolds like a harpy first, then forgets my offenses."

"He was beyond scolding, if you will recall. When you accuse him of lacking honor, you afflict his pride, his self-respect. I would think less of him myself if he truckles down to you on this point. But he shan't. It was done in a public way too, to aggravate the situation. However he might have reacted had you done it in private, between the two of you, his pride will not let him come back now. That is the way men are."

"I suppose you're right," Madeline answered, but in a disinterested voice.

She was not at all convinced she should not write to Eskott. It was apathy more than conviction that stayed her hand. If Eskott called, she would ask him to take her. If he did not come, she would stay home. He didn't come.

Her father dined at home that evening, a thoroughly unpleasant meal, the subject throughout which was the evidence piling up that their cousin was nothing else but an opportunist. All the while he had been working for Fordwich, he had been in touch with the lower elements of the Whig party, it seemed. Now that his reversion to it was out in the open, Fordwich had been subjected to a dozen sly, taunting barbs. "You were too slow in finding the lad a position" and "You can't win them all" was the nature of their comments, for even the Whigs were too polite to say what they really thought: that Fordwich was an old fool, and Madeline had lost her beau to a lady whose uncle was influential in the opposition party.

"Does there seem any likelihood it was Aldred who rifled those letters? That is what I want to know," Lady Margaret said.

"They'll never admit it, but I am satisfied that it is the case. He was seen in private talk with Reed in his chambers yesterday. When Reed came out, the story began propagating. That's the explanation certainly, but as he is to join their ranks as a member, they will hardly blacken his character so early in the game. Give him a year, and he'll do it very capably for himself."

"You underestimate him. It won't take that long," his daughter said grimly.

"Eskott was looking daggers at me across the House all morning. I writhe with shame to face the man. At least we shall be spared his calls at our house in future. Never could understand why he continued coming after Maddie turned him off."

"Maybe it's me he comes to see," Lady Margaret said lightly, for she deemed it high time for some levity to enter the house. "The Old Lady of St. James's Square." She looked a quick peek to her brother to see if this appelation struck him as significant. As it did not, she assumed this part of Madeline's disgrace had not been broadly circulated through town.

"Heh heh, setting up in competition to Lady Hertford, are you Meg?" Fordwich joked. "They may run her down as much as they like. She is a levelheaded woman."

"Does that mean she has talked Prinney into accepting Sidmouth without turning you out of government, Papa?"

"It looks very much like it. Very much like it indeed," he said with satisfaction.

"Good. I am happy to hear it," Madeline said with a wan smile that was not far removed from tears. But they were not really tears of sorrow. Her heart was not broken at all. She was angry and frustrated and ashamed. She was thoroughly chastened, but she was not heartbroken.

Chapter 16

The prince regent accepted Lord Sidmouth's appointment and the Tories were once again securely in the seats of power. There was no further talk of unseating them. The Whigs railed against his perfidy in the House, in the press, and in private, but to no effect. It was back to business as usual. On St. James's Street, too, some semblance of normalcy returned. The major excitement there was the arrival of a card announcing the nuptials of Henry Aldred and Agnes Dannaher.

"I can scarcely credit the gall of this!" Madeline declared throwing it into the blazing grate before Margaret had a chance to see it.

"He hitched his wagon to the wrong horse," Margaret said. "Had he known the prince meant to stick by the old boys, he would no doubt have married you instead of this Agnes person. I was sitting by Taffy Barker's mother at a musical party last evening, and she tells me the girl is plain in appearance, which will please you."

"Plain and *young*, I suppose?"

"Nearly eighteen. Which reminds me, Maddie, we must have a do for your birthday. It is coming up pretty soon. Twenty-six years old, is it?"

"I have every intention of turning twenty-four, and I don't want you telling anyone otherwise."

"Gracious, you'd think you were nudging seventy, like me. Twenty-six ain't so very old."

"It is *ancient*. I ought by rights to be wearing caps, to proclaim my state to the world. Not that I mean to do it!"

"Bah, you're just in low spirits over Henry. You'll get yourself a nice new protégé in the spring, and things will look brighter. You'll see."

"I have abandoned the idea of protégés."

"You must do something with your time. Something more than mere socializing, I mean. If you don't mean to marry and raise a family, all the things that go with it, you will want an exciting hobby."

"Yes," Madeline answered with a little sigh, but in her heart she had no desire to dispense with marriage and raising a family—everything that was natural and attractive to a woman. It had never been her intention to forgo them entirely, only to put them off a little, till the right man came along. She thought increasingly these days that the right man *had* come, but come at the wrong time. When first he asked her, she was too young, not ready for marriage. And on his second proposal, she had been insane, or in love, with Henry. She knew how unlikely it was he would ever ask her again.

She missed Eskott, his frequent visits and easy conversation, his help in arranging the trivia of her daily life, the errands, the opinions and advice. She felt she no longer even understood politics, when she got only one side of the affair being discussed. Eskott had rounded her thinking, shown her that what Papa and his friends spouted as morality was often expediency. It was dull having no arguments, but only unchallenged statements and opinions when a party gathered in the saloon. She missed doing things for him too. When his maternal aunts visited him in March, it was Lady Susan who was seen to show them the exhibits. On another relative's visit, it was not Madeline's tickets for Drury Lane that were borrowed, but Lord Moira's.

She longed to hear his version of the St. Patrick's Day dinner held at the Freemasons' Tavern, when the prince was hissed. Sheridan, she knew, had stood up to defend the prince, but he too had been hissed, and was probably drunk. Eskott would have made an amusing tale of it for her. Papa said only that it was a "shocking disgrace," but she felt it had been roisterously funny, and resented not knowing the truth. Lord Forbes, a Whig aide-de-camp of the prince, had tendered his resignation, and it had been refused. She felt there was some lively gossip in that, too, for Lady Margaret had heard somewhere that Forbes had removed the prince's buttons from his coat, and the lively Whigs would have some amusing anecdotes to relate. But not to her. In her set, it was another "shocking disgrace," and no more. It became clearer to her every day that the lively, interesting, and quite possibly even the more dedicated and public-spirited men did not belong to her father's party.

As if to emphasize it, half the party fell ill with assorted maladies in the last hard spell of winter—old men, whose every sniffle was serious, lest it should carry them off. Her father was amongst them. He was in bed a week, too ill even to be taken home to Highgate, away from city worries. He recovered once more, but he walked at a slower gait, his shoulders more stooped. The next time, he might not recover at all.

As winter waned and spring approached, with the new season looming close on the horizon, Madeline felt her spirits lift, as if stirred to life by the warmer sun, the longer days, the traditional season of rebirth and renewal. She decided she would lay siege to Eskott, to see if she could not beguile him back into being friends with her. The idea was precipitated by her Aunt Margaret's return to Highgate, leaving a large hole in her circle of intimates. At least she had patched up *that* relationship.

On the day of her aunt's departure, she sat down and penned a playful note to Eskott, asking in saucy terms if he was not through punishing her yet. She said she had a set of books that were two months overdue, waiting for him to take them back to the library; her tickets to Drury Lane gathered dust; and she had not been to admire a cathedral since the bishop's last visit. She hoped he would reply in person, and feared he would not acknowledge her letter at all. A card was returned the next afternoon, insultingly late and crushingly terse. He was very busy, and prayed she would excuse his negligence in not calling. He trusted she was well, and signed it with a formal "Eskott."

She read it twice, then tore it up, placed it in the flames, and watched it burn. She felt as though a giant hand were squeezing her heart, causing an ache in her chest. It was all over then. She was so miserable she hardly felt like going out to parties. If Eskott was in attendance, as he often was, he failed to see her, or at most nodded his head in mute greeting, his eyes black, accusing, scornful. At the first large ball of the new season, he chanced to stand directly behind her waiting to be announced. She felt it her golden opportunity to reinstate herself in his good graces, but as often as she turned her head to look over her shoulder, he discovered some other corner of the room to draw his interest. In a fit of pique, she jostled his elbow and said, "Excuse me, would you, by any chance, be Lord Eskott?"

"Good evening, Lady Madeline," he said, without a smile or any display of pleasure. The words fell from his lips like snowflakes—softly, gently, as cold as ice. Then he turned his back to her and began a conversation with the party behind him. Her face pink with shame, she turned to her escort to laugh and talk loudly, and pretend she had not noticed his rude behavior.

The awful subject of Henry Aldred occasionally arose at home. "Aldred has taken his seat in the House," her father told her one evening over dinner. "I hear he has set up in a vulgar mansion in Whitehall, near Taylor's place. They entertain a good deal, folks say. If we receive cards, we will not attend, Madeline."

"That advice was hardly necessary, Papa."

No cards were received. A friend pointed Mrs. Aldred out to Madeline. She was a dumpy girl, extravagantly outfitted with too many feathers on her bonnet. She looked like exactly what she was—a provincial come to town determined to show the ton she could outdo them. She was young, not pretty, but very satisfied with herself, their ages notwithstanding. But how should she complain? *She* had chosen Henry over dear Eskott.

Byron's *Childe Harold's Pilgrimage* was officially launched that March, causing such a stir that Madeline finally got around to reading the advance copy Eskott had thoughtfully supplied her, and she, in her usual dilatory fashion, had not returned. She would have liked a closer acquaintance with the man who said so well what she felt:

What is the worst of woes that wait on age?
What stamps the wrinkle deeper on the brow?
To view each loved one blotted from life's page,
And be alone on earth, as I am now.

But Byron, being an interesting young aristocrat, was a confirmed Whig, so she only had the pleasure of nodding to him at social events.

Her twenty-sixth birthday was an ordeal. She had a party, to please her father, but there was not a guest at the table under fifty. Her father's cohorts and their wives. She did not wish to announce her exact years to her own friends. As the ladies sat around the saloon waiting for the gentlemen to join them after port, Lady Tilsit began outlining a scheme to raise money for orphans.

"We matrons must get together and do something," she said, without even making any little joking reference to the hostess being included in the group in an honorary capacity only. She was assigned the role of a matron, which was as well as saying she was a confirmed spinster.

She could not accept it. She made one last try for some love and romance in her life by carrying on for a few weeks in April with a handsome captain who had returned from the Peninsula covered in medals and ribbons. She tried her hardest to fall in love with him. He was tall and handsome, he was a hero, he was even conversable, interesting for the stories he related of the war in foreign lands, but in the end he was not Eskott, and she could not love him. Captain Townsend was dropped gently but firmly.

She made the arrangements for their annual ball without one bit of pleasure. Doubt as to whether she should send Eskott a card preoccupied her as much as deciding what food to serve and what decorations to use combined. The reason for her indecision was that she had not received cards to his, usually held early in May. She had not actually heard anyone else say they had invitations yet either, and if it were only that he was not having his ball, she would certainly ask him to hers. On the other hand, if he did have a ball and pointedly excluded her name from his list, that was a different matter. She had made enough advances to him. She had no desire to grovel. If only she could chance to meet him somewhere, talk to him, explain . . .

When she received cards from Mrs. Henry Aldred inviting her to attend a masquerade party, she knew just how unwelcome an unwelcome invitation could be. She struck Eskott's name off her list, slowly, sadly. She crossed and crossed it out till there was nothing but a blot of ink on the page where it had been. Then she wrote it again at the top of the list, only to cross it out again the next day, when he was seen on the strut with Lady Susan.

The ball was considered a marvelous success. It was termed a "squeeze," than which no higher praise could be heaped on it. The prince regent dropped around for an hour; two royal dukes attended, six cabinet ministers, the prime minister, and a clutch of the more illustrious Whigs. Madeline had a new gown made up in emerald green to match her eyes. Eskott had always liked her in green. She contrived to get a diamond brooch to stay in her hair by means of a pair of crossed hairpins securing it at the clasp. She wore new white kid gloves up past her elbows, and looked extremely well. Everyone said so, except Eskott, who of course would hardly be expected to attend without a card. She had some little suspicion he might attend on Lady Susan's as her escort. Lady Susan had the same hope, but he declined, and she had to make do with her brother.

The season was at its very zenith. Lady Madeline's engagement book was so crowded she had to scribble in the margins to squeeze in all her appointments. After her own ball, she took the inexplicable decision to go home to Highgate.

"You see Aunt Margaret is complaining of feeling poorly," she pointed out to her father, to have some reason to proffer.

"What, 'Had a touch of megrim the other evening, and went to bed early'?" he read, lifting his brows in astonishment. "That is nothing. You must not lose out on the season only for that. She will be very sorry if you do. Why, you always love the season, Maddie. I remember your first one as though it were yesterday. What high hopes we had, eh? And still have too," he added heartily, seeing the shadow settle in her eyes.

"It seems a hundred years ago."

"You are fagged after the exertion of your ball. Take a day off from trotting. Stay in and retire early this evening. That will set you back up on your pegs."

"Perhaps I shall. And if I don't feel more the thing, then I can always go to Highgate next week," she agreed. She could be swayed by anyone these days. She had got an inch cut off her hair only because the coiffeur suggested it, when she had been trying for a year to let it grow. Nothing seemed to matter enough to argue about.

"I am speaking against the Reform Bill in the House tomorrow afternoon. I thought you would come to hear me. You mentioned you would keep the day open. That will be an easy afternoon for you, sitting and listening."

"Yes, I have it marked here on my calendar."

"I wonder if that is why Eskott didn't show up at our ball," Fordwich went on, his brows bristling in consideration. "He is pushing pretty hard for the Reform Bill. I daresay it is his way of saying what he thinks of my views, without having heard a word of my speech. I rather miss his visits. I though he would use our ball as an excuse to come back. He mentioned last week he was looking forward to it."

Madeline looked at her father, aghast. "You didn't tell me that!"

"Did I not mention it? Yes, it was the first time he had spoken in a month. He has been holding himself very aloof, even in the lobby. There was a deal of gossip about the affair of the letter, and your foolish . . . Naturally he would not want to show the world he took no offense at such Turkish treatment. His pride demands it, but I thought he would come to our ball."

"I didn't invite him!" she confessed.

"Good God! Why not?"

"We didn't receive cards to his, and I—"

"He is holding his off till the fall little season this year."

"You didn't tell me that either."

"I thought you would know it. You hear all the *on dits.*"

"No, I only hear half of them now," she said.

"You soon won't be hearing any of them, if you go on in this slipshod way, not sending Eskott a card to our do. This year more than ever you should have done it, Maddie. We have done him an injury. It is for *us* to make the first step of atonement. Instead of that, you deliver the man another slap in the face. I don't know what has come over you lately," he grouched, but did not wait for an explanation. He was already looking around for his file of correspondence.

Madeline sat down and wrote her aunt half a letter, squeezed it into a wad, and threw it in the wastebasket. There was no fire in the grate. Already it was spring, too warm for a fire. She should have sent Eskott a card to her ball. His speaking to her father was a hint, a reminder that he had not received one. It must have gone against the pluck to have done it. He would not have spoken had he not meant to attend. She had come that close to getting him back, but her pride—vanity—had prevented it. Her life had gone wrong from the moment Henry Aldred had marched into this saloon, strutting and preening and she succumbed to the unutterable folly of thinking she was in love with him.

Chapter 17

The next day was fine enough that Fordwich had his open carriage brought out. Madeline drove with him to Westminster to hear his speech. Maybe she should set up a phaeton and take the ribbons herself. Many of the more dashing ladies in the city were doing so. It would give her a new interest. Eskott would teach . . . Oh, but Eskott could not be asked to do these little chores for her any longer. How difficult it was to break herself of the habit of thinking he could.

She was not the only spectator in the visitors' gallery, but she was one of a small handful. Folks had more interesting things to do on a fine spring afternoon than sit in that dusty, dingy eagle's aerie listening to dull speeches, without even seeing the speaker. There was a long tirade by a member of the opposition, inveighing against the prince's hiring himself a private secretary at two thousand pounds per annum, before her father arose on a new order of interest, the Reform Bill. He was against it, of course. It seemed wrongheaded of him to support a system that sent members of Parliament to represent empty barns or a clutch of one or two families, while vast areas of densely populated terrain had no representation. The county members were elected, but they were outnumbured four to one by the borough members. And even some of the county votes were arranged by one or two great families. Surely that could not be right. Like a child, she had always accepted her father's dictum on it, without giving it a thought. How shallow Eskott must have found her. When she roused herself from her reverie, she saw the visitors in the gallery had dwindled to a pair of young lovers, who were using the privacy of the room to hold hands, and stare out the window toward Vauxhall, probably planning some clandestine meeting at the gardens. She envied them.

Her father finally finished his speech, to mild, one-sided applause. She looked at her watch, wondering if she should wait and go home with him, which might mean sitting for another hour or more in the gloom, or go on alone and send his carriage back. She decided on the latter course as being slightly less boring. She arose and turned toward the staircase, to see Eskott standing, looking at her. It was not his old granite face he wore, but a sober, rather sad one. Her heart raced at the sight of him.

"I have a note from your father," he said, holding out a slip of paper.

"Thank you," she answered, startled. There were a dozen questions in her head. How did Eskott come to be running errands for her father? Had he *offered* to do it? Had it occurred to him she might be present today, when Lord Fordwich was to speak? She did not give voice to any of them, but unfolded the paper and read that she was to go home without her father, as he had a committee meeting with some other members.

"If you need a drive, I am leaving now," Eskott said offhandedly.

"No, thank you. I have the carriage. I'll send it back for Papa. He'll be here for some time."

"As you wish. May, I escort you downstairs at least, call your carriage for you?"

"That would be helpful. Thank you."

Their footsteps sounded hollow on the echoing stairs, slow, measured treads. "You are loyal to spend such a lovely afternoon indoors," he remarked as they descended.

"My father expects it. I must compliment him when he gets home, you know."

"I cannot offer my compliments. He is dead wrong, as usual."

"Yes," she said unthinkingly, her mind busy to find some more interesting topic. She should apologize about her ball.

"Dare we hope you are coming to see the light of reason at last?" he asked with a surprised laugh. He sounded nervous.

"What do you mean?"

"It is not like you to agree with me in these matters, Madeline."

"Oh, but I *do* think Papa is wrong this time."

"Sure you won't come home with me?" he asked, as he opened the doorway into the sun, which seemed blindingly bright. "I have got a new team of grays I am eager to show off; that is why I persist."

"All right. I would like to see them. I am thinking of setting up a phaeton and pair myself."

"I expect Captain Townsend will be happy to teach you to handle the ribbons," he said, with a nod to the stable boy to bring his curricle.

"He has returned to Portugal."

"I had not heard it."

"He was wounded, which is why he was in England at all."

"I thought perhaps he was your new protégé."

The arrival of the curricle and team caused a little stir of excitement. The grays had to be complimented, their points extolled to Madeline. They drove up Whitehall and down Pall Mall toward St. James's Street, discussing politics, while Madeline wondered how to turn the chance meeting to better advantage.

"I was surprised to hear you criticize your father's speech," Eskott said.

"It seems wrong, little boroughs having their own member sent to London." Such members as *Aldred,* she thought, but did not say.

"They are owned by wealthy, influential gentlemen, who appoint their own man."

"Yes, owned by men like you," she answered, to introduce some levity into the talk.

"And Lord Fordwich," he retaliated. "Whigs and Tories alike—we are all active in this borough-mongering. It must be stopped, but till it is, you know, there is no point in not using it to our advantage. Rather ironic when you think of it: we are appointing men to vote themselves out of a job."

"Did you happen to be at the St. Patrick's dinner at the Freemasons' Tavern, Eskott? It turned out a debacle, I hear."

"It had Covent Garden beat all hollow for entertainment. The prince was booed and hissed, and old Sherry, drunk as a skunk, took to his feet to defend him, clutching the edge of the table to keep from falling over. The inebriated defending the indefensible. Marvelous comedy, but deemed poor politics, like so many of poor Sherry's efforts lately. He's a faithful dog— the last of us who *do* defend the prince. His remarks were drowned out in the general booings and hissings. They might have been worth hearing too. Dead drunk he's still a better speaker than most of us. He is dependent on the prince's charity, which is a strong goad to fidelity. Of course, *your* daily reading, the *Morning Post,* whitewashed the affair. Well, bought up lock, stock, and barrel by Carlton House, what can one expect? They found Prinney an Adonis of loveliness, as usual."

"I didn't know Prinney owned a paper!"

"You must have detected the whiff of Hanover in it before now! Pity you had not seen Leigh Hunt's attack in the *Examiner;* it brought the matter into perspective. 'A corpulent gentleman of fifty—a libertine over head and ears in debt and disgrace.' The Hunts were arrested immediately, of course. Brougham will have a field day defending them, with yours truly aiding and abetting him, and likely getting stuck to pay the fine into the bargain."

"I knew there was more going on than I hear at home. They never said a *word* about any of this."

"They would like to pretend it is not happening. There were upwards of ten thousand people in Pall Mall the day of the Queen's Drawing Room, and not one whisper of applause when Prinney went through. Dead silence, ominous silence even."

"I hear Forbes tried to resign."

"It was foolish of Prinney to make him stay on. He went to dinner at Taylor's next night with the prince's buttons and lining removed from his coat, and made a point for everyone to see it. Taylor has fallen out with the prince as well. There is a rumor running around that he tried to seduce

244

Taylor's wife and got knocked down by the outraged husband, but it is only a rumor."

"It's nice to hear all the inside rumors again," she said, hoping to hint him into resuming his visits.

"Subscribe to the *Examiner*," he suggested.

"I will."

"Actually, it's been temporarily shut down pending the trial, but some other sheet will spring up to take its place. Listen closely to hear what rag is being denigrated at home, and you'll know what one to buy."

"I've finally gotten around to reading Byron, and can return it to you now."

"Keep it. I hinted for another from him, and he told me with a pointed smile that the book was also for sale. So I bought a copy, and he autographed it."

They were at the corner of her street, perilously close to home, and still no real rapprochement had been made. "Shall we go on to Hyde Park, or are you in a hurry to get home?" he asked. "These grays need exercise, which is French for saying I want to show 'em off a little in the park."

"I'll be happy to go with you. I must observe all your fiddling tricks, as I shall soon be setting up my own team." This was a definite opening for him to volunteer his services, if he was looking for an excuse.

"Going to set up as a Lettie Lade, are you? I wonder you haven't done it before now," was all he said.

"Do you know of a good pair up for sale? Not *too* wild. I am just a beginner."

"Your father will find something suitable at Tatt's."

In the old days, she would have asked him on the spot to do it for her. The questioning eye he turned to her might have indicated some curiosity in the matter, but there was a little stiffness in him still that held her back. It would be so very humiliating if he refused. "Yes, I'll ask him to make inquiries for me."

They reverted again to items of political and social gossip. The park was busy. They stopped at the barrier to chat with friends, at which time Madeline noticed how many of her lady friends were handling their own carriages. It was strange she had fallen behind them all; she was more usually a leader in matters of fashion. Lady Susan was there, with a tidy team of bays harnessed to a green phaeton.

"Eskott! You see how I am progressing! Driving all alone. Your lessons were most

246

helpful," she said, drawing up beside him. "You were quite right about this pair too. They are a little more frisky than I like, but I am determined to master them. Hello, Madeline." Her eyes were bright with curiosity to see her new flirt with his old flame, but she was too civilized to betray her feelings.

"Is Eskott giving you a lesson?" she asked. "I expect you will be setting up your carriage one of these days."

"I intend to very shortly," Madeline answered, ignoring the first question.

"Is Eskott going to teach you?"

As Eskott said nothing, Madeline said, "No, I shall be learning in the country. I am going to Highgate soon."

"What—rusticating in the middle of the season? Whatever for?"

"For a change," Madeline replied, feeling a fool.

"You are just afraid to drive in the city," Susan chided. "There is nothing to it. I learned in a week. I'll teach you, if you like."

"I would not suggest so perilous a course," Eskott said, speaking to Madeline, but casting a swift, laughing smile at the other lady, indicating some shared incident during their lessons, Madeline was left to conclude. And still he did not offer his services.

"Wretch! How dare you deride my skills!" Susan laughed. "I didn't do a bit of damage to the mail coach."

"I think Lady Elizabeth wants to pass," Madeline was happy to point out, thus forcing Susan to continue on her way.

"See you tonight, Eskott," was her parting speech.

Madeline's heart sank. She understood now why Eskott had not volunteered to help her. He was involved with Susan, more seriously involved than she had heard. His smile, bordering on the sheepish, proclaimed the secret as clearly as words.

"I had better go home now," she said. "We are having company for dinner."

He made no objection, but turned the curricle around and drove her to her door. There was a moment of self-conscious restraint between them as she prepared to leave. Should she invite him to call? Would he suggest it himself?

"Nice seeing you again," was his only remark.

"Thank you for the ride. I enjoyed it."

She turned and began to hurry toward the house.

"When are you going to Highgate?" he called after her, on an impulse.

Angry, disheartened, and frustrated, she called back, "Tomorrow. I leave tomorrow."

"Oh. Then I shall say good-bye now. Have a nice trip."

"Good-bye, Eskott." She blinked back a tear as she wrenched the front door open.

Chapter 18

Highgate Park, stuck off alone in the country, was suddenly the last place in the world Lady Madeline wanted to be. Why had she said such a stupid thing? She wanted to buy the liveliest team in town, set up a dashing high-perch phaeton, much higher than Lady Susan's. She wanted to buy six new gowns, none of them white, and find herself a handsome new flirt. If she could induce Lady Margaret to come to town, it would be an excuse to stay. She wanted to break out of her father's fusty old Tory circle and make friends in the livelier Whig aristocratic group. Eskott was not the only gentleman who could educate her, let her know what was really going on in the city. There was the handsome new poet, Byron.

She took no conscious notice that her strange lethargy was dissipated. She only knew she wanted to be doing things again. The first thing to be done was to find an excuse to remain in town. She dashed off a letter to her Aunt Margaret, first outlining how enjoyable a season she was missing, then added a fact more likely to bring her aunt running: Lord Fordwich was not well. He was assigned a recrudescence of his cold, coughing dreadfully, poor man, and he would not curtail his work in the least, hard as his daughter tried to make him. "That should do it," she said aloud as she sealed it up and set it aside to await her father's frank.

If Lady Susan was seeing Eskott that night, as she obviously was, there was no doubt where they were going. Lady Susan's best friends, the Donaldsons, were having their annual ball. Madeline had cards for it, had even sent in her acceptance some days ago, when she was drifting around in a cloud, not knowing what she wanted. She did not normally wear the same gown twice within a short space of time; but as Eskott had not seen her new emerald green, she wore it again, with again the diamond clasp in her hair, and the elbow-length white gloves. She admitted modestly, as she whirled in front of her mirror, that she looked quite ravishing. It was ridiculous to feel old when she was only twenty-four, going on twenty-three.

She went to the ball with her spirits soaring, determined to win Eskott back, and received two surprises. Eskott was not there, and Henry Aldred and his bride were. The trip to Scotland must have been canceled. Such a lack of decorum in Henry did not surprise her. Once he had landed his lady, fulfilling any promises made would not occur to him. The creature had the gall to present his simpering wife to her, to tell the girl this was his former patron "about whom you have heard so much."

"Don't believe all you hear, Mrs. Aldred," she advised, in the coolest accents she owned.

Henry laughed lightly, refusing to take offense. "I have told Agnes she must call on you," he persisted.

"What poor advice to give your bride," she answered. "You know we only receive Tories at the Second Court of St. James, Mr. Aldred."

"You receive Lord Eskott," he pointed out, making a joke of it.

"True, but his advanced years appeal to me. We *old ladies,* you must know, insist that all our callers be dry behind the ears. Good evening, Mr. Aldred, and Mrs. Aldred." She turned and strolled nonchalantly away.

"She's marvelous, isn't she?" she heard Henry say in a loud voice. Demmed jackanapes!

Her next item of business was to discover why Eskott was not present. She walked up to Mrs. Donaldson and asked in a spirit of polite disinterest, "I thought Lady Susan would be here, ma'am. She must be ill, if she is missing your ball?"

"Ill? Oh no, she is acting hostess for Eskott's dinner party. They will all be along shortly."

Madeline had suddenly had enough of the ball. *She* should have been his hostess. The honor was always offered to her when his aunts declined. That the role was Susan's was too ominous an event to be considered in this public place. She must find Papa and go home.

"It is hardly worth having the horses put

to, if we are to stay for under an hour," he grouched.

"I have a headache, Papa. I'll go home alone if you want to stay."

"I *don't* want to stay. I told you I did not want to come at all, but you insisted."

"If you don't want to stay, then let us leave," she said, resigning in her temper.

She wished she had not posted her letter to Aunt Margaret. She *would* go home tomorrow. She would not stay in town and have to smile her congratulations when the match between Eskott and Lady Susan was announced. Humankind could bear only so much in one season.

"Wait till Saturday and I'll run down with you for the weekend," her father suggested when she told him of her decision in the morning.

"Very well."

The team and phaeton were a diversion. She'd get them when she went home, if she got them at all. One of the grooms would teach her to handle the ribbons, on the privacy of country roads. She had the modiste in to discuss designs for a new outfit to wear when she set up her carriage, to get in the day. She took lunch alone, rifling through copies of *La Belle Assemblée* to select other patterns for autumn wear. She was just arising from the table when Eskott came pelting in, without disturbing the door knocker.

He looked pale, shocked, *awful.* "What's the matter, Eskott?" she asked, running forward.

He took her two hands in a tight grasp. "You haven't heard?"

"No, nothing. What is it? Is it Papa?" she asked, deciding that only death could have shaken him so.

"No, Perceval. The prime minister has been assassinated, shot through the heart."

"Oh, my God! Who did it? How did it happen? When?"

"In the lobby of the House of Commons. I saw it. A man ran up to him, a madman, deranged. Before anyone could stop him, he raised his pistol and shot him through the heart. He didn't get away. He was apprehended before he could run. I can't believe it. It's—it's like a melodrama on the stage. It was awful."

"The poor man. Oh, this is dreadful. What a confusion Parliament will be thrown into, *again.*"

"Bellingham is the assassin's name, they say. He had been in prison in Russia, it

254

seems, and our representative there did not help him. He was bankrupted over the business. It affected his brain certainly. It was our representative from Russia he wanted to kill, but he was not around, so he shot Perceval instead. It's incredible. I hoped I would catch you before you left. You are going to Highgate today . . ."

"No, I had decided to wait till Saturday. Papa asked me to. The trip will be off now of course. He'll have to stay in town. There will be meetings . . . It was kind of you to take time to come and tell me."

"That's not really why I came, Maddie," he said, in a softer, hesitant voice. "Let us sit down. We must talk. I think you have some idea what I want to say."

She could not speak for the lump in her throat. A gentleman to the end, he was going to tell her he was engaged to Lady Susan, before she heard it in some public place. He took her hands in his, holding them tightly. She swallowed down the lump and replied, "Yes, I have a pretty good idea, Eskott."

"There's no use fighting it, is there? I know I should be angry with you: you have treated me with abominable disregard for years, culminating in that outrageous accusation! How *could* you say such a thing to me? What really hurt was that you could believe such treachery of *me,* but not of *him.* "

"A madness most indiscreet. I have paid for it, and will go on paying."

"You're not telling me you still care for him!"

"Good gracious no! I nearly slapped his face last night when he came bowing up to me, with his simpering bride in tow."

"I am ashamed to be in the same party as him, but at least he takes a very inactive part. He is turning brewmaster, I hear."

"I can't believe I ever cared for him. But love is blind, they say."

"It is infatuation that is blind. Love sees the flaws only too clearly, but goes on caring just the same, in spite of all," he said with a rueful smile that made her wonder if his mind was unalterably set on Lady Susan.

"Then I am disinfatuated. I see only the flaws now. I don't even find him handsome. The best part of him is his jacket, and I made him order that. He doesn't merit a Weston jacket."

"He doesn't merit any more remorse either, Maddie. Life is too short."

"Yes," she said, thinking of poor Perceval, cut down in his prime. "I must make the most of what is left. Do something useful and worthwhile."

"Helping the poor, making the world in general a more just place?"

"Yes."

"Welcome to the party," he said, taking her fingers and squeezing them. "You'll make a perfect Whig hostess. Converts are always enthusiastic partisans. That woolsack I'll be sitting on one of these days is big enough for two. Care to join me?"

"Lady Susan . . ."

"I did such a poor job of hiding my disappointment last night when I learned you had left the ball that she gave me my congé on the spot. She said it was kind of me to *try* to fall in love with her. Wasn't that sweet? I was so happy I kissed her. The two of us received congratulations from half a dozen bystanders."

"Well they should congratulate you. She's a lovely girl," Madeline said with a surge of affection for the hussy.

"I am a fool to let her slip through my fingers. I want to make my position absolutely clear this time. I am not here to resume my role as your delivery boy-cum-convenient escort. I am thirty-five years old. I realized when I saw Perceval shot today how tenuous a hold we have on life. He was only fifty. He little thought when he tied his cravat and shaved this morning that he would never do those things again. It could have been me that got the bullet as well as he, for the assassin was quite obviously deranged. I don't plan to waste another day of my life. It's marriage immediately, or the end of our relationship. This is the third time I've asked you. Three and you're out. What do you say, old girl?"

"I would be honored to join you on the woolsack, dear Eskott. Or anywhere else."

"Good, I have a few other places in mind as well," he said, pulling her into his arms. She felt safe and warm and loved, and every bit as excited as a bride-to-be should feel on such an occasion. She was entering a new phase of her life, her "boys" left behind, their place taken by one fully mature man. When he kissed her, the past fell from her mind and she envisioned a bright future, in which helping the poor played a much smaller part than loving dear Eskott.